THE 12 SCREAMS OF CHRISTMAS

GOOSEBUMPS®
Also available as ebooks

ALSO AVAILABLE:

IT CAME FROM OHIO!: MY LIFE AS A WRITER by R.L. Stine

Goosebumps®

MOST WANTED

SPECIAL EDITION

THE 12 SCREAMS OF CHRISTMAS

R.L. STINE

SCHOLASTIC INC.

ISBN 978-0-545-62777-1

Goosebumps book series created by Parachute Press, Inc.
Copyright © 2014 by Scholastic Inc.

All rights reserved. Published by Scholastic Inc., *Publishers since 1920.*
SCHOLASTIC, GOOSEBUMPS, GOOSEBUMPS HORRORLAND, and associated logos are trademarks and/or registered trademarks of Scholastic Inc.

12 11 10 9 8 7 6 5   15 16 17 18 19/0

Printed in the U.S.A.   40
First printing, October 2014

PROLOGUE: 1882

"Give me my cap!"

My little sister, Flora, made a wild grab for her cap. But Ned swiped it out of her reach. "Give it back to me, Ned," Flora said. "I mean it."

My name is Abe Marcus. Ned and I are identical twins. We look exactly alike. Even Ma and Pa can't tell us apart. But we don't act alike. I am the serious twin. Maybe it's because I am two minutes older.

Ned pulled the floppy cap down on his head and took off, running around the parlor, laughing like a madman. Flora chased after him, grabbing for the bright red cap with both hands.

Ned loves to tease Flora and play jokes on everyone. He is always getting into trouble and making people angry and being noisy and causing a ruckus.

At our old school, Ned poured molasses in all the inkwells in our classroom desks, and no one could write a word for weeks. He was sent home by the teacher for a talk with Ma and Pa. But they were so busy getting ready for our move to this new house, they didn't have time to punish him.

Ned and I are twelve, and Flora is eight. She is the baby of the family, and Ma says she is as spoiled as four-week-old buttermilk.

Ned told Flora she smelled like sour buttermilk, too. And Flora grabbed him around the waist and started to tickle him in the stomach with both hands. Ned is very ticklish, and Flora wouldn't let him get away. She tickled him until he burped up some of his lunch, and Ma finally made her stop.

Flora is tiny, but she's a terror.

That was at our old house. Now, here we were on our first day at the new house. Flora was chasing after Ned, darting through the moving crates stacked up in the parlor.

Ned started to wave the red cap in the air over his head, shouting, "It's mine now! All mine!"

"I'm warning you, Ned Marcus. I'll tickle you again if you do not give me back my cap!" Flora cried.

That made Ned stop. I told you, he hates being tickled. I think he'd rather have a tooth pulled. He crinkled the cap between his hands, then he tossed it at her.

Flora growled at him and jammed it down over her dark, wavy hair. All three of us have dark, wavy hair. But you never see Flora's hair,

4

because she wears that floppy, ragged cap day and night, even to the dinner table.

"Keep your smelly hands off my cap," Flora warned Ned. "You're just jealous because you don't have a cap. And because you and Abe have to share a room, and I have a room of my own."

"Ned and I don't mind sharing," I said. "Because we never had a room of our own before. Remember? We had to sleep in Ma's sewing room."

"My room is better than yours," Flora sneered. "I am going to have linen curtains as soon as Ma can go into town and buy the fabric."

"We don't want curtains," I said. "Curtains are for girls."

Truth is, Ned and I were *thrilled* to move into this new house. It was a hundred times bigger than the little cottage we lived in before. It had stairs that led up to a second floor and an attic above that. We never had stairs before. And we had a large backyard that stretched to a fence at the end of the property.

The backyard had lots to explore. There was a white-shingled garden shed, some kind of falling-down shack, a chicken coop, and an old stone well near the back fence.

We couldn't wait to celebrate Christmas in the new house. Pa said he would cut down a fresh pine from the woods down the block. I could already picture it decorated with popcorn and cookies and lighted candles.

When we first saw the new house, Ned's eyes went wide. "Are we rich?" he asked.

Pa never laughs. But he actually chuckled when Ned said that. "We're far from rich, son," he said. "But we should be just fine here."

Pa is a stonecutter. He has so much work, he hired two apprentice stonecutters to work for him.

Now, here we were, Ned, Flora, and me, exploring every inch of the new parlor, the clear glass windows, the wide fireplace with its tall mantel.

We heard a loud thud. I turned to see Pa backing into the room. He and Mr. Powell, our new neighbor, were carrying in the couch. Hoisting the couch in both hands, Pa nearly backed into Ned. "If you're not going to help, at least get out of the way," Pa said.

"Can we explore the backyard?" Ned asked.

"Yes, can we?" Flora and I said together.

"Not you," Ned told Flora.

"Why not?" she demanded angrily, hands pressed to her waist.

"Because you're too ugly. You'll scare the birds," Ned said.

"I'm *not* as ugly as you," Flora shot back. "You scare the sun every morning. That's why it hides behind the clouds."

I burst out laughing. Flora is a poet sometimes.

Pa and Mr. Powell set the heavy couch facing the fireplace. Pa adjusted the straps on his denim overalls. "Flora, go help your mother in the kitchen," he said. "There is much to unpack."

Flora made an unhappy face. Then she tugged her cap down lower on her head, turned, and hurried to the kitchen.

Pa squinted at Ned and me. "Okay. Go out back and explore. But wear your coats. I think there's snow on the way." He sniffed the air. "I can smell it coming."

"And better stay away from that well near the fence," Mr. Powell added. He was a big, red-faced man with straight, straw-colored hair. His stomach bulged under the bib of his overalls.

"That well is deep," he said. "And the stone walls are crumbling. It could be very dangerous."

Ned and I didn't wait for any more warnings. We pulled on the sheep's-wool coats Ma had made for us and ran through the kitchen, where Flora and Ma were opening a big moving crate. Then out the back door and down the steps, into the wide yard with its tall grass and weeds swaying from side to side in the gusting wind.

We couldn't hold in our excitement. We let out loud yips and skipped over the grass, cheering for our new freedom, our new life.

We had no way of knowing it was going to be the worst day of our lives.

2

Gray clouds covered the afternoon sun. The air felt cold against my face. Two fat crows perched on the fence at the back of the yard. They cawed loudly as Ned and I ran and skipped over the tall grass.

We took turns hopping over a stack of firewood logs. We pulled open the door to the narrow garden shed. It smelled of fertilizer inside. A rusted wheelbarrow stood tilted against the back wall. Some kind of animal had chewed a ragged hole in one of the floorboards.

"What about that shack over there?" Ned said, motioning toward it with his head. "Let's look inside it."

The little shack reminded me of a gingerbread house my grandmother made one Christmas. It was a perfect, square little house — until Flora accidentally sat on it. She crushed one whole side of the roof. Ma turned it around so the crushed side didn't show.

The shack behind the garden shed was falling down, too. It was probably built before our house was. But it had gone to ruin. A lot of the shingles were missing. Green moss covered one wall. The window beside the entrance was cracked.

Ned started running to it, but I held him back. "Pa said not to go there," I said. "He said it might be haunted. That's what he heard in town. Something bad happened in there. And now it's haunted. That's why no one has lived in there for lots of years."

A smile spread over Ned's face. His dark brown eyes flashed. "It's haunted, Abe? Let's *go!*" he exclaimed. "Let's chase out the ghosts."

He was always braver than me. I couldn't let on that I was afraid of ghosts. Pa used to tell us ghost stories before bedtime when we were Flora's age. Ned loved them. But hearing about headless ghosts returning from the grave to find their heads, or restless spirits that clanked and howled at night — hearing those stories gave me nightmares.

Ned picked up a long stick from the grass and walked toward the old shack, pretending the stick was a cane. I followed close behind, my eyes on the broken window and the darkness beyond it.

As we stepped into the shadow of the little house, a chill swept down my back. My skin tingled. Were there ghosts inside? Were they friendly? Or did they hate intruders?

The wooden front door squeaked and nearly fell off its hinges as we pulled it open. A sour smell greeted us as we stepped inside.

"Ooh, something died in here," I said. I pinched my fingers over my nose.

"We could fix this up and live back here," Ned said, gazing around. "Our own little house."

"Are you crazy?" I said. "It's filthy. Everything is covered in dust. And it's falling apart. Those ceiling boards are cracked. They'll probably fall on our heads and crush us."

Ned laughed. "Are you afraid, Abie? You are — aren't you. Look. You're trembling."

"I am not," I replied through gritted teeth.

We were standing in a tiny, bare front room. No furniture. No lanterns for light. Outside, the storm clouds lowered. The room grew darker, nearly as dark as night.

The floorboards squeaked as Ned and I made our way to the next room. A small bedroom. A narrow cot stood against one wall. Its canvas was ripped down the middle.

"It smells even worse in here," I whispered. I felt my stomach start to churn.

"Think about it," Ned said, peering out the cracked window. "If we clean it up, we could have our own house right in the backyard." He forced open a door. Behind it, I saw a small closet.

The putrid odor was really making me sick.

"I . . . think we should leave now," I said. I turned and started walking out of the bedroom.

And that's when I heard it. That's when I heard the ghost's harsh whisper. It seemed to be coming from the open closet.

"Welcome . . ." I heard. "Welcome. Welcome to your DOOM."

3

"No!" The word burst out of me in a choked cry. I could feel a chill tighten the back of my neck.

"Welcome to your doom, Abe." The raspy whisper again.

I turned back. My eyes searched the darkness of the tiny bedroom. Suddenly, I realized what was happening.

"Ned!" I cried. "You . . . you fooled me again!"

He burst out of the closet laughing and slapped me hard on the back. "You catch on fast, Abie."

I raised my hands to wrap them around his neck and strangle him. But he danced away, still giggling.

He loves scaring me. And he's very good at it.

He picked up the long stick and swung it at me like a sword. "Do you believe in ghosts, Abie?"

"Of course I do," I said. "Everyone believes in ghosts." I started to the front door. I wanted to get out of there. But I was turned around and found myself in another small room in back.

This room had a low wooden chair with one of its legs missing. And a wide dresser, covered in at least an inch of dust. An oval-shaped mirror hung above the dresser. The glass was so stained and cracked, I couldn't see myself in it.

"It's hard to believe people actually lived in this shack," I said. "Why do you think it's been empty so long?"

Ned tapped the dresser with his stick, sending up a wave of dust. "Too many ghosts, I guess," he said. He started to say more, but he stopped.

We both heard the sound. A loud hum. No. More of a buzzing sound.

"What is that?" I said, tilting my head to listen harder.

"I think it's coming from the front room," Ned said, pointing with his stick.

I stumbled over a crack in the floor as I followed him to the front.

The sound rose, then fell, a little like an ocean wave.

Gray light washed in through a dirt-caked window. The room was bare. I spotted something high in one corner up near the ceiling. The buzzing grew louder as Ned led the way across the room.

We stared up at the large, gray, oval-shaped object. It appeared to be stuck up there.

"What *is* that?" Ned whispered. He raised the stick and poked the middle of the object.

A mistake.

I saw the big black insects fly out, buzzing louder.

Ned must not have seen them. Because he poked the nest again. And now a raging sound surrounded us as dozens of wasps angrily shot out and began darting in wide, crazy circles above us.

Ned turned to me, a confused expression on his face, the stick still raised. "Are those wasps?"

"I think so," I replied. I'd never seen a wasp's nest before. But I'd seen drawings of them in a science book at school.

As the big insects raged and swarmed and buzzed, I grabbed Ned by the shoulder. "Run!" I cried.

I gave him a hard push. The two of us stumbled to the door. The furious sound followed us.

"They're chasing us!" I screamed.

I reached the door first and shoved it open with both hands. My shoes hit the ground running. Ned was running at my side, his eyes wide with terror.

I turned back and saw the dark cloud of wasps, rising and falling against the gray sky, soaring toward us. "We . . . made them . . . angry," I gasped, struggling to breathe.

The wasps shot over us, so many of them they blocked the sky.

"Run! Run!" Ned cried.

He didn't need to say it. I was running harder than I'd ever run, heart pounding, throat so dry I started to choke. But we couldn't outrun them.

The black cloud lowered over us. The furious buzz rattled in my ears.

"Owww! I'm *stung*!" Ned screamed. "Help! Abie — they're *stinging* me!"

I ducked my head. Wasps attacked my back, my shoulders, my chest. I swatted at them, swinging my arms frantically.

"I'm stung!" Ned screamed. "Oww. My neck."

I grabbed his shoulder and pushed him forward. "Keep your head down," I rasped.

The garden shed came up in front of us. I grabbed the door, heaved it open, and we fell inside. I pulled it shut. And the two of us stood there in the darkness, breathing in the sour odor of fertilizer, wheezing, shaking, our whole bodies shuddering.

I could hear the wasps outside, hear them circling the shed. I heard their bodies bumping the wooden shed walls as if trying to force their way in.

Bump bump bumpbumpbump. It sounded like a hailstorm, pounding the little shed.

Ned and I stood there listening, trembling, afraid to make a sound.

How long did it take for the angry swarm to move on? Probably a minute or two. But it seemed like *days*.

Finally, the sound faded. We could hear the wind again.

But we didn't move. Ned scratched his neck. "That really hurt," he murmured.

I grabbed the door handle and slowly . . . slowly pushed the shed door open a crack. I peeked out, ready to slam the door shut if I saw any wasps.

But they had moved on.

Ned and I stepped out of the shed. The nasty smell followed us. It was on our clothing, on our skin. But I didn't care about that. We had escaped a hundred stings.

I turned Ned around and examined his neck. He had a round red bump where a wasp had stung him.

"We're safe!" Ned cried happily. "Hey — we outsmarted those wasps! Are we clever? You bet we are!"

He slapped me on the back. Then he jumped onto a low stone wall that zigzagged through the yard. He started to do a Ned dance. That's what I call the crazy, flapping, arm-waving, shoe-tapping dance he does.

I laughed and joined him on the low wall. I can't dance the way Ned does. My arms and legs just don't fly around the way his do. But I started to dance, too.

Shouting and laughing, the two of us did a celebration dance, a dance to celebrate escaping
those swarming wasps.

But the celebration didn't last long.

Flora's shout broke into our laughter. "Look!"
she cried. "I can dance, too."

Ned and I stopped our dance. I jumped off the
wall. We turned to the back of the yard. And we
both started to scream in horror.

"No, Flora! Get off there! Get off the well!"

"Flora — jump off! Get off! Don't climb on the
well! You're going to fall!"

5

She tossed back her head and laughed. From under her cap, a strand of her wavy black hair fell over her forehead.

"I can dance, too!" She kicked up her shoes and started to do a jig, grinning at us, her dark eyes glowing.

"No, Flora — please!" I cried. "Please!"

Ned and I both froze in horror as she slipped. Her arms flew up over her head. She opened her mouth in a deafening scream of horror.

Kicking her feet, she dropped into the well. She made a desperate attempt to grab the top of the well wall with both hands. But they slid right off and she dropped out of sight.

The last thing I saw was that floppy, red cap.

Ned and I both gasped when we heard the splash. It sounded far away, deep at the bottom of the well. The most chilling sound I'd ever heard.

"Ohhhh." A moan of horror escaped my open mouth.

19

Ned and I flew to the well. I leaned over the edge and peered down. "Flora? Flora? Can you hear me?" My voice echoed, sounding deep and hollow as it traveled down to the bottom.

I heard shouts. Ma and Pa were running out from the back of the house.

"What happened?" Ma cried. Her long gray skirt scraped over the grass. Her hands were clasped in front of her apron. "Where's Flora? What happened?"

Pa ran up to Ned and me at the well, his face grim, his lips tight together. Ma hung back, wringing her hands. Her lips were moving in a silent prayer.

"Flora — we'll get you out!" Pa screamed. "We'll save you. Can you hear me? We'll save you!"

I squinted down to the well bottom. The dark storm clouds overhead made it difficult to see. But I could hear Flora splashing in the water down there. Wild, frantic splashes.

I could see her red cap, gray in the dim light, bobbing and spinning.

And I heard her high, shrill screams: "Get me out! Get me *out*!"

"Do something! *Do* something!" Ma shrieked, her hands knitting around each other.

Pa blinked. I could see the fear in his eyes.

My stomach had tightened into a knot. My throat closed shut. I had to force myself to breathe.

"Get me out!" Flora's voice sounded so tiny and far away. The splash of the water down at the well bottom grew faster, more frantic.

"I . . . don't have a rope long enough to reach her," Pa said. I saw tears form over his eyes.

"The bucket!" Ma screamed. "Send it down. Send the bucket down to her!"

Yes. The bucket. She could grab on to it and we could pull her up.

Pa snapped out of his panic. He leaned over and grabbed the bucket off the well wall. He lowered it into the well. Then he grabbed the iron crank at the side of the well with both hands and began to turn it.

"Flora! Can you hear me?" he called, his voice trembling. "I'm sending the bucket down. Grab on to it."

"Get me out!" Flora screamed.

"Hold on to the bucket. We'll pull you up!" I cried. I listened to my voice echo down to the bottom. I was sure she heard me. She *had* to hear me.

Pa cranked and the thick rope moved, lowering the big wooden bucket to the bottom. His face reddened as he cranked as hard and fast as he could.

"Grab the bucket! Grab the bucket!" Ned and I shouted down to our sister.

Pa uttered a groan as we heard the bucket splash down.

Squinting, I could see the bucket bobbing in the ink-black water. And I could see Flora's cap and then her hands wrapping around the top of the bucket.

"Hold on!" I cried. "Hold on! Pa will pull you up!"

Pa lowered his shoulders to the crank. "She's coming up," he called to Ma. "I'm pulling her up." His face was bright red and tears rolled down his cheeks.

He turned the crank with both hands, strained at it, tugged it as fast and hard as he could.

"Hold on!" I called down to my sister. "Hold on, Flora. Pa is pulling you up."

Ned let out a cheer. Flora, gripping the sides of the bucket, was halfway up. Pa cranked harder. She was sliding up. Her dress was soaked, sending a trail of water to the bottom.

"Hold on! Hold on! You're almost here!" I cried.

I gasped when I heard the sharp *snap*.

I knew immediately what had happened. I saw the stub of frayed rope. I saw my sister and the bucket start to drop.

"The rope broke!" Pa wailed. He still had his hands on the crank.

The rope had snapped. And the three of us stared in silent horror as Flora plunged back down the well, hitting the water with a splash that sent up a tall wave.

"Do something!" Ma shrieked.

"We don't have a long rope!" Pa cried. "We don't have anything to pull her up. Maybe Mr. Powell down the road? I could jump in the carriage and —"

"No time," Ma murmured, shaking her head. "No time, Pa."

Ned and I stared at each other, mouths open, holding on to the cold stones.

And from down below, Flora's terrified voice rang in my ears:

"Get me out! Get me out! Get me out! Get me out! Get me out! Get me out! Get me out! Get me out! Get me out! Get me out! Get me out! Get me out!"

PART ONE

DECEMBER, THIS YEAR

Okay, I was late. It happens.

But I didn't want to be late this afternoon. I knew my friend Jack Hopper was waiting at my house. He was doing me a favor, helping me rehearse. And I needed the help. I really wanted to get this part in the middle school Christmas play.

But sometimes fate is cruel.

I wrote that on my Facebook page a few weeks ago. I'm not sure why. A bad mood, I guess. My friend Carol Ann made me delete it. She said, "Kate, it's too dark. And you're not a dark type of person."

That's true.

I'm Kate Welles. I'm twelve and I'm not a flake or a rah-rah cheerleader type. But I'm usually the cheerful one in the group.

Except when Courtney Smith is around. Courtney was the reason I was late getting home.

She and I got into an argument after school. Don't even ask me what it was about. Face facts. I'm always getting into arguments with Courtney. Seriously. She's the definition of the word *frenemy*.

Well, Mrs. Wentz — good old Mrs. Wentz with her good posture and short blond-highlighted hair and orange lipstick that doesn't suit her at all — she doesn't like to see her sixth graders fighting in the hall. (Actually, I like Mrs. Wentz despite her lipstick and her weird laugh that sounds like she's puking.)

But she stomped into the hall and separated Courtney and me. And when we couldn't remember what we were arguing about, she made us stay after school to think about it.

Of all days to be late. My house is pretty far from school. But Mom doesn't like to drive in snow, so I had to walk.

The ground was covered with four or five inches of snow, and the wind had blown drifts along the curb nearly up to my knees. It was the first snowfall for my new Ugg boots, and the one on the right was pinching my toes.

Aren't your feet supposed to be the same size as each other?

The sun was out. The snow had ended that morning. But the wind was lifting sheets of snow off the ground and swirling them around me.

My parka was covered in tiny snowflakes. I kept rubbing my nose because it was numb from the cold.

The play auditions were scheduled for after dinner at the school. It was already four o'clock. Not much time to rehearse with Jack.

I decided to take the shortcut home.

This wasn't an easy decision for me. I brushed snow off my forehead and stared at the cemetery gate. Was I really desperate enough to cut through the cemetery?

Well, in a word, yes.

When was the last time I took the shortcut through this old graveyard? In the fall, just before school began.

That's when I had the most frightening moment of my life. Seriously. The most surprising and the most frightening.

I hadn't dared to come back this way since. In fact, I always walked two blocks out of my way to avoid the cemetery.

I squinted through the iron gate and saw a scrawny gray squirrel standing erect — erect as Mrs. Wentz — on a snowbank, staring back at me. His tail stood up straight. He didn't move a muscle.

Did he think I couldn't see him?

"Don't ever play hide-and-seek," I called to him. "You'd stink at it."

That sent him scampering over the snow. I watched him till he vanished behind a tilted gravestone.

I gripped the iron gate, wrapping my gloved hand around the frozen handle. I could feel my heartbeats pick up speed. My whole body shivered.

Kate, what happened last fall won't happen again.

I talk to myself a lot, but it seldom does any good. I'm a tense kid. I know it. But I have good reason to be tense.

The gate was stuck in a snowdrift. I kicked snow away, then tugged with all my strength. Finally, I swung it open wide enough for me to slip inside.

It won't happen this time.

It won't.

I took a deep breath and sidestepped into the graveyard. It took me a while to find the path through the graves. The snow rose and fell in hills and valleys. The gravestones had tufts of snow on their tops, as if thick white hair had grown there.

The snow crunched under my boots. I wanted to walk fast, but I kept slipping and almost losing my balance.

The wind had been blowing, swirling the snow. But it suddenly stopped, as if someone had flipped a switch and turned it off.

The new silence made me gasp. Now the only sounds were my shallow breaths, puffing up white steam in front of me, and the steady crunch of my new boots on the snowy path.

I kept my eyes straight ahead. I tried not to look at the crooked rows of snowy gravestones on both sides of me.

In front of me, the afternoon sun had lowered. I raised one gloved hand to my forehead to shield my eyes from the blinding glare.

And that's when I heard the first low moan.

Like an animal groan from deep in its throat.

At first, I pretended I didn't hear it. I kept my head lowered, my glove shielding my eyes, and trudged steadily forward.

A second moan made me stop. And then in the windless silence, I heard the chatter of whispers, hushed, raspy voices, muttering and moans and murmurs.

I couldn't help it. I opened my mouth in a cry of horror.

Because I knew it was happening again.

I turned to the voices. I couldn't stop myself.

I squinted at the graves, and I saw them again. Pale, gray figures. I could see right through them.

The first one that caught my eye was a little girl. She couldn't have been more than five or six. Wearing a tattered gray smock that came down to her ankles. She stood barefoot in the snow. Her long hair fell over her forehead. I couldn't see her face at all.

Did she have a face?

I saw two men huddled in long overcoats, their heads frozen inside oval blocks of ice. Faces buried in ice, but their lips were moving as if they were having a conversation.

Two sad-looking women in long black gowns, shaking their heads, shaking, just shaking them. They were barefoot, too, like the little girl. Only they floated six inches above the snow, floated in the air.

Others perched on their tombstones, faces torn, eyeballs glassy, moaning, moaning up at the bright blue sky.

I saw two children, the saddest of all. The boy in short pants, his bare legs as white as the snow. He had long icicles hanging from his chin. The girl rocked back and forth on her feet, as if she couldn't find her balance. She wore a tattered short skirt and gray sweater. Her head was tilted to the sky, and she was crying, sobbing loudly, holding the boy's hand and wailing.

Frozen to the spot, gaping in horror, I saw at least a dozen of the sad creatures, maybe more. Some floated above the low hills of snow. Others were half buried in the ground.

Ghosts. All of them. Cemetery ghosts. And I could see them.

I didn't move. I didn't take a breath. I watched them, my eyes moving from one sad, ugly creature to the next. I could see them so clearly.

And I realized that I could no longer ignore my special power. I could no longer pretend that I was just a normal sixth-grade girl. I could no longer ignore the frightening truth.

I can see ghosts.

It happened before. The first time was at a fifth-grade gymnastics meet. Then, last fall, it happened right here in this old graveyard.

That's where I saw the sad children and the pale, mournful-looking adults floating up from their graves. Huddling together, murmuring and whispering, chattering to each other.

I tried to shut it away, shut it from my mind. I pretended it didn't happen. And I stayed away from the graveyard. I never came near it.

Why? Because I didn't want to be weird. I didn't want the kids at school to laugh at me and tease me and get on my case.

Too late for that.

Courtney and some other kids already call me Ghost Girl. Why? It's a long story. It started at the fifth-grade overnight last spring.

I never should have told them what I saw there that night. I should have known that no one would believe me. I should have known they would tease me and laugh at me and never let me forget it.

Ghost Girl.

Well, I was definitely seeing ghosts now. Shivering in the middle of a graveyard. The wind picked up again. It appeared to blow right through the ghosts huddled near their graves. They shook and shivered like me.

I let out a sharp cry when I realized they had all turned away from each other. Now they had their sad, sunken eyes on me.

They stared in silence. Even the little kids.

I could see them and they could see me.

My whole body tingled, not from the cold. I

prepared myself to run. Would my legs work? Was I frozen to that spot on the snow-covered path?

I heard whispers over the howl of the wind.

"She can see us."

"She is watching us."

"What does she want? Why is she here?"

A tall, bearded man in a black overcoat ten sizes too big for him, the sleeves nearly down to the ground, took a silent step toward me. His eyes were wide and glassy. He staggered stiff-legged.

Stay away. Please — stay away.

I thought I spoke the words. But I only thought them.

My brain was frozen. I suddenly felt so helpless. I wanted to move. I wanted to turn and run. But my legs wouldn't cooperate.

I stood there trembling as the tall, bearded ghost staggered toward me. And as he moved, he stretched out his arms. Stretched them out stiffly. As if reaching for me.

His hands were big and bony. Almost like skeleton hands. His fingers twitched as he held the hands straight out in front of him, ready to grab me.

And still I couldn't move.

What strange hold did the ghost have on me? Did he have some supernatural power to keep me in place?

As he drew nearer, I could hear him grunting. Low grunts like a pig makes when it's eating.

Gronnnk grunnnnk grunnnnk.

The ugly sound sent chills down my back.

Move, Kate. Run!

The ghost lurched up to me. He raised his hand. He slid his bony finger down the side of my face.

And I started to scream.

"Kate — what's wrong?"

"Huh?" I jumped as the voice rang out over the swirling cemetery winds.

"Kate?"

The tall, bearded ghost vanished. They all vanished. Disappeared into the piles of cold white snow.

I spun around. "Jack?"

He wore a maroon hoodie over his faded jeans. A black leather jacket. His boots tossed back snow as he ran up to me. He pulled back the hood, revealing his straight, copper-colored hair. The sun made his blue eyes glow.

"Jack? What are you doing here?" My voice came out shrill and high.

"Trying to find you," he said. "Are you okay? Why did you scream?"

I didn't want to tell him the truth. He didn't believe me last spring, and he wouldn't believe me now.

"I . . . uh . . . got some ice in my boots," I lied. "No biggie, dude."

He brushed snow off my shoulder. "You sure you're not seeing ghosts again?"

I shook my head. "Why would I see ghosts in a graveyard? That's the last place I'd look."

"You're weird," he said. Then he added, "In a good way."

"Best compliment I had all day," I said. I raised my gloved fist and we bumped knuckles.

We started to walk toward my house. I kept glancing back. The ghosts didn't return.

"How did you know to find me here?" I asked.

He pulled the hood over his head. "I went to school. I thought maybe you were there. I ran into Carol Ann. She said she thought she saw you walking in this direction."

"Courtney made me late," I explained. "She started an argument with me, and we were shouting at each other a little. You know how it goes with Courtney. And guess who comes by? Mrs. Wentz. She doesn't like shouting. She kept us there for almost an hour."

"Where's Courtney?" Jack asked.

"Who cares?" I said.

He chuckled. We reached the gate on the other side. Jack grabbed the latch and pushed the gate open. I could see my house at the end of the block.

I turned back one last time. The graveyard stood empty, the snow swirling down the rows of gravestones. No ghosts. I still shivered.

"I thought you and Courtney were friends," Jack said, closing the gate behind us.

"Not anymore," I said. "I kind of hate her. Well, I don't really hate her. I just detest her a little."

We both laughed. I can be pretty funny. When I'm not scared out of my mind seeing ghosts no one else can see.

"Seriously," I said. "She's just so mean to me. I guess that's why I want to beat her out for this part in the play. I just want to win something, you know?"

He nodded.

"I just need a little bit of good luck," I said.

As I said that, a dark shadow slid over the snow in front of me. It took my eyes a few seconds to focus and see that it was a large black cat. Its yellow eyes glowed as it stared up at me. It pulled back its lips, baring its fangs, and hissed.

I grabbed Jack's arm.

"What's wrong?" he asked.

"That cat," I said. "It hissed at me."

Jack squinted into the snow in front of us. "Cat? What cat? Are you freaking out or something?"

I sucked in a sharp breath. Jack couldn't see the black cat. That meant the cat was dead. A ghost.

It hissed again. Its eyes were locked on mine.

"Just a shadow," I said to Jack. "The sun glare off the snow is so bright. Guess I'm seeing things."

He nodded and kept walking.

The black cat vanished behind a snowdrift. I realized I was shivering.

I had just said I needed some good luck. And then the ghostly black cat appeared. Did that mean I was about to have *bad* luck?

10

"A ghost! There's a ghost in the house!" I cried. "Doesn't anyone care?"

Jack shook his head. "You don't sound frightened enough."

I laughed. It was kind of funny — since I've had a lot of experience with ghosts and screaming.

We were in my den, rehearsing for the play tryouts. First, we had warmed ourselves with steaming mugs of hot cocoa. Then we had closed ourselves in the den to act out the brother and sister roles in the script.

The den is my favorite room in our house. It has floor-to-ceiling bookshelves on three walls. A fireplace with soft, comfy green leather couches and armchairs facing it. And a beautiful antique piano in one corner.

Dad wanted a flat screen TV above the fireplace. Dad would like to have a giant TV in every room. But Mom put her foot down and said the den should be a quiet, peaceful place.

I tried the line again, making my voice more shaky. "A ghost! There's a ghost in the house! Doesn't anyone care?"

Jack frowned. "Not frightened enough, Kate," he repeated. "I think you need to scream. I mean, you and I are all alone in this old house, and we've just seen a ghost on the stairs."

"Then you should scream, too," I said.

"Boys don't scream," he said.

"They do in horror movies," I replied.

"No way," Jack said. "I'm not going to scream here. Look at the script. It doesn't say I should scream."

"What are you two arguing about?"

My mother strode into the den, carrying a bowl of nacho chips. She took a chip, then set the bowl on the coffee table in front of the couch.

My mom is the kind of person who can eat just one chip. When she was in her twenties, she was a fashion model in New York. She is still thin and as pretty as a model, with big blue eyes, a dramatic helmet of short blond hair, high cheekbones, and perfect, smooth skin.

I know what people think when they see the two of us together. They think *what a shame Kate looks like her father instead of her mother.*

Or am I being a little crazy?

"Well?" Mom said. She nibbled at the nacho chip, making it last.

"We're not arguing," I said. "We're rehears-ing." I waved the script in the air. "We have tryouts after dinner for *The 12 Screams of Christmas*. Remember? I told you about it? It's Mr. Piccolo's Christmas play?"

She chewed some more. So far, she'd only eaten half the chip.

Jack grabbed up a handful of them and began jamming them into his mouth, crunching loudly.

"Mr. Piccolo, right," Mom said. "He's your music teacher? What a perfect name for a music teacher."

I rolled my eyes. "Good one. No one ever thought of that before, Mom."

She made a face at me. "Kate, were you *born* sarcastic?"

"No. I took a class," I said.

That made Mom and Jack laugh. I told you, I'm pretty funny.

"Tell me about the play," Mom said, finally fin-ishing her chip.

"Mr. P wrote it," I said. "It's got all these songs in it."

"And it's supposed to be scary," Jack said, reaching for another handful of nacho chips.

Mom blinked. "Huh? A scary Christmas play? You mean like Dickens's *A Christmas Carol*?"

"Kind of," Jack said. "It's about a family who moves into a haunted house on Christmas Eve.

The house is haunted by a ghost family who used to live there. But they had a terrible tragedy that ruined their lives. And now they want to celebrate Christmas and keep the new family there forever."

Mom had turned her eyes on me. "It's a ghost story," she said. "Kate, you know you have a thing about ghosts. Are you sure you want to be in this play?"

I gasped and the script fell from my hand. I bent to pick it up. "Mom, I don't have a *thing* about ghosts," I said. "I —"

Jack laughed. "What about at the fifth-grade overnight last spring?"

"Are you really going to bring that up again?" I cried.

"Kids still call you Ghost Girl because of that night," Jack said. "Seriously. You totally lost it."

I wanted to punch him. I could feel my face growing hot and knew I was blushing. "I can't believe we're still talking about this," I muttered.

"Kate, calm down," Mom said, taking a few steps toward me.

But I was too angry. "I don't care if anyone believes me or not about that night," I said, curling and uncurling my fists. "I really did see a ghost in that tree."

"Kate, please —" Mom tried to stop me.

"It was an old man, and he was sitting on a tree limb, smoking a pipe, and watching us."

Jack shook his head. "It turned out to be a white plastic trash bag."

"It *did not*!" I said. "I saw what I saw. I don't have a ghost *thing*, Mom. I saw a ghost that night. I — I —"

I was about to tell her and Jack about the ghosts I'd just seen in the graveyard. And about the hissing black cat.

Somehow, I stopped myself. I held myself back. They wouldn't believe me no matter what I said. And Mom would just repeat that I shouldn't be in the play since I have a *thing* about ghosts.

"Can we change the subject?" I said. "Can we —"

I stopped midsentence. I froze because the piano in the corner began to play. All by itself. No one there.

I stared at it in horror as the music filled the room. Stared at it — and opened my mouth in a shrill scream.

11

"Kate? What's wrong with you?" Mom cried. She spun away from me and hurried to the piano. "That's my ringtone," she said.

She picked her phone up from the piano and held it toward me. "See? It's not the piano. It's my phone."

She gave me one more concerned look. Then she raised the phone to her ear and walked out of the den, talking to someone.

Jake was watching me from the couch.

Did I feel embarrassed? Did I feel like a total moron? Three guesses.

I wanted to follow Mom out of the room and shout at her: "Of *course* I have a thing about ghosts. Because I can *see* ghosts!"

But what was the point of that?

I raised a finger to my lips. "Don't say a word, Jack. Don't say a word about the piano, hear?"

"Okay, okay," he said. He made a zipping motion over his mouth.

I glanced at the silver clock on the mantel. "Can we get back to the script?"

Jack took another handful of chips. The bowl was nearly empty. "Didn't you say Courtney would come over and rehearse with us?"

"Oh, right. Guess I forgot to invite her."

He frowned at me. "How come you and Courtney are so messed up? I thought you were good friends. You've known her since kindergarten, right?"

I rolled my eyes. "Don't rub it in."

Jack shrugged. "I just don't understand —"

"She's always on my case," I said. "She's the one who started calling me Ghost Girl. She's never forgiven me for making us lose that state gymnastics meet."

"You mean last year? When you thought you saw another ghost?"

I smacked the rolled-up script across his leg. "I don't want to talk about it. I fell off the balance beam, remember? I could have broken my neck. But no one cared about that. They were only upset because I lost the match for the team."

"Because you thought you saw a ghost in the bleachers," Jack said.

"Whatever."

I really wanted to stop this ghost talk. I liked Jack. I didn't want him to think I was loony.

"Courtney thinks she's so much better than me," I said. "And now here we are, trying out for

47

the same part in the Christmas play." I let out a sigh. "I just have to win — for once. Just once."

Jack scratched his head. "I think you're taking it all too seriously."

I rolled my eyes. "Well, thanks for your support."

Does he have a crush on Courtney? I wondered.

"Let's practice screaming," I said. "That will impress Mr. P. We have to scream like we're terrified out of our shoes." .

"Okay, Kate. You go first."

I took a deep breath — and opened my mouth in a shrill scream. I cut it off and made a choking sound as I saw the figure float into the den.

A girl. All white. Her face, her arms, her flowing dress. Her hair fell to her shoulders, white, white as snow. She didn't appear to see Jack and me. She floated past the piano, her pale arms raised at her sides, floated silently, easily.

I jumped to my feet from my chair, holding my breath, my eyes on the ghostly girl.

I turned to Jack. His eyes were following the pale, floating figure.

"Jack," I whispered. "Do you see her, too?"

12

The ghostly girl laughed. "You like my ghost makeup? I made you scream — didn't I?"

"Courtney!" I cried. "How —"

"Your mom let me in," she said. Her long white gown flowed around her as she crossed the room to us. "I thought I'd give you a little surprise." Courtney laughed again. "Ghost Girl, you look terrified!"

"I . . . I wasn't screaming because of you," I stammered. My heart was still pounding in my chest. "Jack and I were rehearsing. Practicing our screams."

Courtney dropped down on the couch next to Jack. Her face was caked with white makeup. And now I could see that she was wearing a white wig. She was white from head-to-shoes, except for her light brown eyes.

She smiled at Jack. "My sister Chloe's friend is a makeup artist. Look at me. It took over two hours to do this. Seriously. Think Mr. P will be impressed?"

I slapped the rolled-up script against my palm. "It's not really fair," I said. "Mr. P didn't tell us to come to the tryouts tonight in costume."

"I wanted to do a little extra," Courtney said. She brushed the end of the white wig behind her white shoulders. She turned to Jack. "You know, since the gymnastics team bombed out — thanks to Kate — I decided I want to be an actress. I'm serious. That's why I really want to get this part in the play."

She was talking only to Jack, as if I wasn't in the room.

He stared at her but didn't reply.

I didn't know what to say. Courtney knew that she and I were competing for the same part. So was my friend Carol Ann.

Did she really think she could steal the part by showing up in ghost makeup?

"You two go ahead," she said. "I don't need to rehearse. I've got the part down." She tapped her temple with a pale white finger. "It's all in here."

I bit my bottom lip. I fought to keep my anger down. *She thinks she has already won the part*, I thought. *She thinks it's a done deal. Well . . . I'm going to surprise her. I'm going to be the winner. I'll do anything to win that part. Anything.*

13

It would be funny if Mr. Piccolo resembled a piccolo, but he doesn't. Actually, he's quite round. More like a bass fiddle. He has a big pouch of a belly that stretches the oversized turtleneck sweaters he always wears.

He has a round face, too. He's mostly bald and his scalp shines like a bowling ball. He wears square eyeglasses, which are always sliding down his long, straight nose. He peers at you over his glasses with his little sparrow eyes.

He reminds me of an owl that should go on a diet.

He has a high voice and a nervous way of talking really fast. I guess it's because he gets very excited about everything we do in his class.

Most everyone likes him because he's kind and patient and never makes you feel bad even when you totally mess up a song or act up in class. And because he's always so *up*, so enthusiastic and gung ho.

He greeted us at the auditorium door as we trooped in for the tryouts. I counted at least twenty kids, mostly from our music class, but some from the seventh and eighth grade, too.

The snow had stopped but the temperature had dropped into the teens. We tossed our winter coats and parkas and hoodies onto chairs at the back of the auditorium. And we kicked the snow off our boots before following Mr. P up to the front.

I hugged myself to stop my shivers. I had layers on, but I should have worn a heavier sweater. Down the long aisle, some kids were grouped around Courtney, admiring her ghost makeup and costume.

I looked around. She was the only one in costume.

Across the aisle, my friend Carol Ann flashed me a thumbs-up, and I returned it. "Break a leg!" I called to her. She shook her head hard, brushing snow from her coppery, curly hair.

It was cold in the auditorium. I hoped it would be warmer onstage.

"People. People!" Mr. P called, clapping his hands. "People — follow me. Let's take a seat on the stage."

He bounced down the aisle. It looked like he had a beach ball under his yellow turtleneck. He snapped his fingers as he walked. He always had some kind of rhythm going.

He sat down on a canvas director's chair and waited for us to get seated in front of him on the stage. I wanted to sit next to Jack, but Courtney plopped down between us.

The auditorium was dimly lit, but the stage lights were on. Kids were chattering and laughing. But I stayed quiet. I kept going over the lines for the tryout. I didn't know them by heart. I had the script rolled up in my backpack.

Mr. P raised his hands to get everyone quiet. The bright stage lights made his glasses gleam like silver. He shielded his eyes with one hand.

"Before we start the tryouts," he said, "maybe you'd all like to hear a true ghost story. It happened right here in this auditorium. Did any of you know that this auditorium is haunted?"

Before anyone could answer, Courtney spoke up: "Don't freak out, Kate. Maybe you should cover your ears."

That got everyone laughing. I guess they all knew how I lost it last spring at the overnight.

I could feel myself blushing. I pretended to laugh, as if she'd made a terrific joke. Then I gave Courtney a playful shove — only I didn't mean it to be playful.

Mr. P leaned forward in his canvas chair. "This story happened more than eighty years ago," he said. "A boy named Cliff went to this school. Cliff was a sickly boy. Very frail. In very bad health. But his dream was to be in the school play."

Mr. P shoved his glasses up on his nose. His eyes swept over us. I guess he was making sure we were paying attention. We definitely were. The auditorium was silent except for the hum from the furnace vents along the walls.

"Cliff won the starring role in the play," he continued. "But he was so weak, he could barely make it through rehearsals. The doctors said Cliff shouldn't be in the play. They said he was too frail and sick.

"But Cliff argued with his doctors. He said being the star of the play was his biggest dream, and he wouldn't quit for any reason."

Mr. P pushed his glasses up again. He shifted his weight in the narrow chair. "The play was given right here on this stage," he continued. "And guess what? Cliff was amazing in it. He gave a wonderful, powerful performance, as if he wasn't sick at all. It was like the performance had given him new strength, new life.

"It was a triumph in every way. When it ended, the audience cheered and clapped and made Cliff take a second bow."

Mr. P cleared his throat. He swept a hand back over his bald head. "After the show, everyone wanted to congratulate Cliff and tell him how great he had been. But . . . no one could find him. They searched the dressing rooms backstage. They searched the whole school. But no sign of Cliff.

"Finally, the drama coach telephoned Cliff's home. After several rings, his mother answered. Her voice trembled. She sounded as if she'd been crying. She said: "I'm sorry Cliff couldn't be in the play tonight. It was his dream, but he didn't make it. He died yesterday morning."

I let out a gasp. A hush had fallen over the stage. No one moved or made a sound.

Mr. P took a long pause. Then he said: "Yes, I see that you understand. Cliff came up on this stage and performed the play *one day after he died.*"

He paused again. Then: "The show must go on. That's what Cliff believed. Ever since that night, ever since that ghostly performance, we leave the last seat in the top row of the balcony for him. Sometimes, actors onstage look up — and they say they can see Cliff in his seat, watching their play. Others have said they've seen him walking on the stage. Many people believe that Cliff's ghost refuses to leave this auditorium."

I couldn't resist. I turned and raised my eyes to the balcony.

Dark up there. No lights were on. The only light washed up from down below.

But squinting up to the last row, I moved my eyes to the very last seat. And saw something move there. Was it a face? Yes.

Looming from the shadows. A face. A boy's face. And then I could see the outline of his body. Could see him lean forward, his eyes on the stage.

My breath caught in my throat. I raised my hand to my forehead. And gasped. "Cliff? I see him. Cliff? Is that you?"

14

"No. It's me — Paco!"

The voice rang down from the top of the balcony.

I sucked in a breath. Laughter burst out all around me. The laughter echoed off the walls of the empty auditorium. Everyone was laughing, even Mr. P.

"Way to go, Ghost Girl!" Courtney slapped me hard on the back.

I wanted to hide. I wanted to die. I wanted to fall off the stage and disappear through the floor below. I'd never been so embarrassed. My face was blazing hot. My hands started to shake.

It was just a ghost story Mr. P made up. And I fell for it.

Of course, there was a good reason for that. But, still, I looked so stupid.

Mr. P slid off the chair and stood waiting for everyone to settle down. When they finally stopped hooting and laughing at me, he waved a hand up at Paco. "For those of you who don't know," Mr. P said, "Paco is a seventh grader. He is on the tech squad for our play. He'll be in charge of sound and lighting."

"Kate will be on the ghost squad," Courtney chimed in. It wasn't very funny, but kids started laughing at me all over again.

"Okay, get off the stage, people," Mr. P said, shooing us with both hands. "I want you to take seats in the auditorium till I call you up for your tryouts. We'll do the tryouts for Livvy, the sister, first."

We all started to the steps at the side of the stage. Jack stepped up beside me. He patted my shoulder. "Don't let Courtney get you upset. You'll do an awesome audition."

I shrugged. "Whatever." I started down the steps.

Behind us, Mr. P stopped Courtney at the edge of the stage. "I'm very impressed with your costume," I heard him say. "And the excellent makeup job. I appreciate your extra effort, Courtney. Why don't you stay up here? You can be the first audition."

Another victory for my friend Courtney. It was nothing but *win win win* for her tonight.

And for me . . .

Suck it up, Kate, I told myself. *Stop feeling sorry for yourself. Jack is right. You'll do a killer audition.*

I took a seat in the second row next to Carol Ann. She squeezed my wrist. "Are you nervous? I am."

I nodded. "A little."

"I have one more announcement," Mr. P called from the stage. "And it's important. When you're up here, don't bump any controls, and be careful to stay away from the trapdoor at stage right." He pointed. "It seems to be opening and closing on its own. Someone is coming to fix it tomorrow."

He squinted down at me. "Kate, maybe there *is* a ghost in here." And then he said, "Would you do me a favor? Would you go downstairs to my office and bring up my clipboard? I left it on my desk."

"No problem," I said, jumping up. I squeezed my way to the aisle past Carol Ann and some other kids and started to the exit at the back of the auditorium.

I heard Mr. P call Jack to the stage to audition with Courtney. I didn't want to see Courtney's tryout. I was glad to have an excuse to miss it.

I wanted to concentrate on my own. As I walked, I went over Livvy's lines for the hundredth time.

It was a little after eight o'clock. Through the school doors, I could see a bright half-moon high in the sky. The moonlight poured across the hall floor, making it glow an eerie blue color.

The school was deserted. Half the lights in the hall were turned off.

I walked by the sports honor display case across from the darkened principal's office. The silver trophies gleamed dully through the glass. I passed posters for the annual school auction and annual coat drive.

The stairs were at the end of the hall just past the study hall. Most of the lights were off. The stairway was blanketed in deep shadow. I held on to the metal railing and took the stairs slowly.

Only two ceiling lights were on downstairs, dim as candles. A chill ran down my back as I walked toward Mr. P's office at the end of the hall. It was cold down here. The air felt heavy and wet.

Our school is old. The windows all leak cold air from outside. So the rooms and halls are always chilly.

The floorboards creaked under my shoes as I walked. I stopped when I heard a groan. Very nearby. It took me a few seconds to realize it was the furnace kicking on.

My footsteps rang out in the silence. The door to Mr. P's office stood open. The office was totally dark.

I gasped when I saw someone leaning against the wall.

Squinting into the shadows, I realized it was a ladder. I laughed out loud. *Kate, stop scaring yourself.*

I stepped into Mr. P's office and fumbled on the wall for the light switch. I felt a chill at the back of my neck. Why was I so tense? Probably because of the tryout.

The ceiling light flashed on, and I gazed around the office. I saw the clipboard on the side of the desktop. As I leaned to pick it up, something caught my eye.

It was a sheet of notebook paper with a handwritten list on it. It seemed to be a cast list with the names of all the characters in the play on it. Next to their names, I saw scribbled kids' names.

Next to Gerald, the brother in the play, I saw Jack's name. And next to Livvy . . . ? My hand shook. I brought the paper closer. Next to Livvy, the lead sister, I saw Courtney's name with a question mark after it.

Had Mr. P already cast the play? Had he decided who got the parts before the tryouts?

My eye went down to the bottom of the page. My name was there, along with Carol Ann and three other kids. Did that mean he thought we could possibly win parts? Or did that mean we were out?

He would never decide everything before we had a chance to try out, I told myself.

That would be unfair. Mr. P is always the most fair teacher in the school.

I set the paper down on the desktop. My eyes roamed around the office, looking for anything else that might be interesting. He had a photo-graph of a yellow-and-black cat framed on his desk. And a stack of sheet music in front of it. The window ledge held several big pots contain-ing prickly-looking cactus plants.

I realized I was spending too much time here. I picked up the clipboard, started to the door, then stopped. "Hey!"

The office door was closed.

I didn't remember closing it. Squeezing the clipboard in my hand, I stared at the door. Solid wood painted navy blue.

The hall was very breezy. Did the wind push the door closed?

I stepped up to the door and wrapped my hand around the brass doorknob. I turned it and pushed. "Whoa."

The door didn't budge.

I tried it again. Twisted the doorknob the other direction. Pushed hard. Then pulled.

A chill ran down my back.

"Hey, somebody!" I shouted. "Somebody!"

The door was definitely locked. Someone had locked me in.

15

I pounded my fist on the door. "Hey — who's there?" I shouted. "Let me out! Somebody — let me out!"

I pressed my ear to the door and listened. Silence in the hall.

The door didn't lock itself, I knew.

"Hey — let me out!" I screamed. I dropped the clipboard and pounded the door with both fists.

No answer.

I stood there, breathing hard, my heart racing.

The school was empty. No one else was down here. No one could hear me.

I crossed my arms in front of me and started to pace back and forth across the small office.

Who locked me in here?

I stopped in front of the window. I had an idea. If I moved the cactus plants aside, maybe I could push the window open and escape.

I picked up the pot in the middle of the window ledge and set it down on the floor. "Whoa." The tall cactus rested in a bed of stones. The thing weighed a ton.

I shoved the next cactus plant to the side, careful not to get stuck on its spiky thorns. I'd made enough room to climb out — if I could shove the window open far enough.

I bent and grabbed the bottom with both hands. I tugged. I let out a groan as all my muscles strained. It didn't move.

I tried again. I couldn't get the window to budge. A lot of the old windows in the school had been painted shut or were just stuck.

I gave it one more try, then backed away. A sigh escaped my throat. It seemed like a good plan, but the window just wouldn't move.

I crossed to the door and pounded some more. "Is anyone there? Can anyone hear me?"

Silence.

I tried the door one more time. Then I spun away from it and dropped into Mr. P's brown leather desk chair.

Someone will come for me soon, I told myself. *They'll miss me. They'll see that I'm not back, and they'll come for me.*

I put my elbows on the desk and propped my head in my hands. And waited, staring at the round clock above the door. Five minutes passed. Ten . . .

They have to notice that I didn't come back with the clipboard.

Fifteen minutes passed. I started to pace back and forth again. "This is ridiculous," I said out loud.

Then I had another idea. "How stupid can you be, Kate?" I cried.

My cell phone. I'll text Jack to come get me. I grabbed at my jeans pockets.

Wait.

My phone was in my backpack. My backpack was upstairs in the auditorium.

Standing in the middle of the room, I heard someone jiggle the door.

I gasped in relief. "Finally!" I cried, and called out, "Get the key. The door is locked."

A few seconds later, the door swung open. Jack blinked at me, his face twisted in surprise. "You're still here?"

"Of *course* I'm still here," I said. "I was locked in. What took you so long to come down here?"

He squinted at me. "Mr. P sent me down for his clipboard. We thought you left."

"Excuse me?" I cried.

"Courtney told everyone you weren't feeling well, and you went home."

16

My mouth dropped open. I saw red. I actually saw a curtain of red in front of me. Red anger.

"Courtney said you texted her and told her you were sick and going home," Jack repeated. "You missed your audition. They're doing the mother and father now."

"I . . . I don't believe this," I stammered. "That liar!"

Jack picked the clipboard up from the floor. "She probably —"

I didn't give him a chance to say another word. I couldn't hold it in any longer. I opened my mouth and shrieked. Howled in anger.

"Should I kill her *now*?" I cried.

I dove forward, pushed him out of the way, and bolted out of the office. My shoes thudded the floor, the sound echoing like drumbeats. My hands were clenched into tight fists. My whole body throbbed with anger.

The cheat. The liar.

Did she really think she could get away with that?

"Kate — slow down!" I heard Jack far behind me. "Take it easy. Kate — wait up!"

No way I'd wait up for him. I shot up the stairs, taking them two at a time. Breathing hard, I ran the short distance to the auditorium and burst through the door.

I raced down the aisle toward the stage.

Courtney? Where are you? Where?

My vision was blurred, still red from my anger. I spotted her onstage. She was acting a scene with the kids who were trying out for the mother and father.

Heads turned as I thundered to the stage. Carol Ann called out to me, but I ignored her.

I bolted up the steps at the side of the stage. Mr. P was watching Courtney and the other two kids. But he spun around as I came exploding toward him.

"Kate? I thought —"

I ran up to Courtney, my fists tight at my sides. "You . . . you locked me in — didn't you!" I gasped. "You locked the door!"

Her eyes went wide. She started to deny it. But she couldn't keep a smirk off her face. She couldn't stop a smile from spreading across that white ghost face.

"Kate, what is the problem?" Mr. P said, climbing down from his canvas chair.

I could feel my whole face start to burn as I exploded in rage. I let out a furious scream. I grabbed Courtney around the shoulders and shoved her backward. Then I lowered my hands to her waist and dragged her to the floor.

"Unh." She grunted in surprise and tried to push me away.

But my anger made me strong. I'd never been in a fight in my life. But now I was out of control, a different person, a person in a mad rage.

"Get off me!" Courtney cried.

But I rolled on top of her, pressing her back to the floor, and pulled her hair as hard as I could with both hands.

"Stop this. Stop this at once!" I heard Mr. P cry, his voice shrill and high.

Kids shouted and screamed.

Mr. P reached down for me. But I rolled away from his grasp. Held on to Courtney, squeezing her waist.

"Get off! Kate — are you crazy? Get off!"

I held on to her, and we rolled over the stage floor, rolled and wrestled, punching at each other.

I heard the screams grow louder. I heard people crying, "Stop! Stop!"

But I didn't see the open trapdoor until it was too late.

I felt a wave of panic as I realized the floor had given way. Courtney rolled over me, and we fell.

"Nooooo!" I screamed as we dropped into darkness.

We fell, holding on to each other. Fell fast and hit the bottom hard. I felt the air leave my body in a whoosh. My chest collapsed. And everything went black.

Even though I had stopped falling, I could feel myself sinking into a deep blackness. I could feel myself being pulled down, down ... as if I was being swallowed, swallowed by the cold darkness.

Slowly, I forced my eyes open. My head throbbed. Pain shot up and down my whole body.

I struggled to raise myself up. It felt as if the darkness, so heavy, was pushing me down. I blinked several times, trying to clear my head. But my temples pulsed with pain.

Finally, I saw Courtney, hunched beside me. Her hair fell over her face.

"Where are we?" My voice came out in a whisper.

She brushed the white wig back with both hands. "I don't know. Somewhere in the basement."

Courtney climbed to her feet. She straightened her long white ghost skirt. She brushed back her hair again.

I raised a hand for her to help pull me up. But she turned away from me. She began walking into the blue-black darkness.

"Courtney — wait," I called, still in a whisper. "Where are you going?"

She didn't answer. She kept walking, the skirt scraping the floor. She was fading, as if stepping into a thick fog.

"Courtney — wait up! I can't see you," I called, finally finding my voice.

"You've ruined everything, Ghost Girl," she called back. "You've done it again. Just like the gymnastics meet. You've ruined everything."

"But, Courtney —"

She vanished.

I gazed into the blackness all around. Silence.

I stood up. *There's got to be a way out of this basement.*

I took a step, then another. If I could find the wall, I could follow it till I came to a stairway.

And then another thought entered my mind: *They all saw Courtney and me fall through the trapdoor. Why hasn't anyone come down to rescue us?*

Stumbling in the darkness, I found the wall. I pressed my palm against it. It felt cool and smooth. Slowly, I began to walk, sliding my hand along the wall.

I turned a corner. The blackness lifted a little. The basement opened into milky-gray light. I kept my hand on the wall but started to walk a little faster.

Suddenly, I realized I wasn't alone.

I stopped and squinted into the gray glare. Someone stood up ahead in the middle of the hall.

"Hey!" I called out, my voice echoing down the corridor. "Did you come to help us?"

No answer.

I took a few steps forward. Slowly, he came into focus. Paco. The boy from up in the last row of the balcony.

"Paco?" I cried, walking quickly. "I'm glad to see you. I'm kind of lost and —"

I stopped with a sharp intake of breath. As he came closer, I saw that he wasn't standing on the floor. His shoes . . . They floated three or four inches in the air.

He stood with his hands at his waist, dark eyes glowing. Floating above the floor without moving.

"You . . . you really *are* a ghost," I stammered.

His straight black hair fell over his eyes as he nodded. "Yes, I am, Kate." His voice was soft, breathy like a whisper of wind. He brushed back his hair. His eyes burned into mine.

"What are you doing down here? What do you want?" I said. I turned my head to avoid his stare. It felt like a hot beam invading my brain.

He reached out a hand. "You'll see. Come with me."

71

I took a step back. His stare was frightening me. But he floated closer and grabbed my hand. "Come with me," he repeated in that breathy whisper.

"I don't *want* to!" I screamed. I struggled to free my hand. But his grip was too strong.

"Let go!" I cried. "I don't want to come with you. Where are you taking me? Let *go*!"

18

I couldn't pull free. I couldn't escape. He grasped both of my hands and tugged me through the inky gray light.

It took me a few seconds to realize he had pulled me off the floor. I was floating, too. Fear choked my throat. I pleaded with him to explain, my voice nearly as hoarse as his.

"Please — Paco. Stop. Where are we going? Why are you doing this?"

He didn't answer.

I was gripped with fear. My mind leaped from thought to thought. *Why didn't Mr. P and the others come down here to help Courtney and me? Where is Courtney? I saw Paco around school all the time. How did he become a ghost?*

He pulled me around a corner. We floated together six inches off the floor.

Suddenly, I heard voices. Mumbles. Low whispers. I couldn't make out the words. The murmurs circled me. I twisted and turned and tried to see who was speaking.

Bright lights flashed on.

"Oh!" I cried out as I saw faces. Dozens of faces.

Paco and I were in the middle of a large room jammed with people. He let go of me. My eyes gazed from face to face.

I knew at once there was something wrong with them. The faces appeared to shimmer in and out of the light. Their skin was yellow and stretched tight. Their eyes were glassy and rolled crazily in their heads.

I saw children in tattered clothes, stained rags. Old men, their chins wobbling up and down but no sound coming out. Women with long, scraggly strands of hair falling from bald, rutted heads.

Ghosts.

"Paco," I whispered, huddling close to him. "These people are ghosts."

He nodded. He motioned with one hand. "Kate, you stared at them in the cemetery."

I swallowed. "I . . . what?"

"You stared at them. You disturbed them." He brought his pale face close to mine. "You disturbed them *a lot*."

His words sent a shiver down my back. "I . . . don't understand," I stammered. "Why are they here? Did they follow me to school? What do they want?"

It took him a while to answer. The ghosts pressed in closer, tightening their circle around Paco and me. I could smell them now, smell the decay of their clothes, the stale odor of their skin.

Their eyes were all locked on me. Unblinking. Wide-eyed stares. Mouths hanging open.

"What do they want? *Tell* me!" I screamed.

"Kate, they want you to audition," Paco said finally.

"Huh?" I blinked. I felt another cold shiver.

"They want you to sing," Paco said. "Sing the '12 Screams of Christmas' song from the play."

"No," I whispered. "Get me away from here, Paco. I won't do it. I won't."

The ghosts began to murmur. Some shook their heads. Some jumped up and down.

"Oh, look," Paco said. "You're making them angry, Kate."

The ghosts moved even closer. They practically bumped up against me now. The odor was overwhelming. Their mouths jabbered up and down. Their cold stares made me shut my eyes.

"You have to do it, Kate," Paco insisted. "If you want to get back upstairs, you have to sing for them. Go ahead. Now."

All around me, the ghosts began to chant: *"Sing sing sing sing . . ."*

The chant rose to a horrible roar, an ugly rumble from deep in their hollow chests. *"Sing sing sing . . ."*

"Okay!" I cried. "Okay! Please — stop!"

The chanting cut off instantly.

I turned to Paco, my heart pounding. "If I sing for them, will I be able to go back to the others? Will you show me how to go back upstairs?"

He nodded, his dark hair falling over his face, hiding his expression.

"Okay," I said again. I started to run the words to the song through my head. Could I remember them all?

The ghosts stood in silence now, not moving. They slid back a few feet, as if to give me room to sing.

I took a deep breath. And I started the song. *"On the first day of Christmas my true love screamed, 'I see . . .'"* I stopped with a gasp.

No voice. I had no voice. The words escaped in a choked whisper, so softly even I couldn't hear them.

"Try again," Paco urged. "Hurry."

I took another breath. And started the song.

No. Not even a whisper this time. It felt as if someone was squeezing my throat shut. I struggled to breathe.

I opened my mouth to try again. *"On the first day of Christmas . . ."*

No. I mouthed the words but no sound came out.

What's happening? Why can't I sing?

The ghosts' blank expressions turned to anger. Once again, their murmurs became a roar.

They moved as a group. Closed in on me. Tightened the circle until they bumped against me. Their mouths sliding up and down, eyes rolling, they raised their hands. Like marionettes on strings. They raised their dead hands in front of them.

"Ohhhhh." I let out a moan as a cold hand brushed my cheek.

"Paco — help!"

But he had vanished. Disappeared into the angry mob of ghosts.

I was helpless. Surrounded. Another ghost's hand scraped my forehead. Another cold hand brushed my cheek.

Hard hands grabbed my shoulders. They began pulling me down . . . down . . .

I shut my eyes and started to scream.

19

I couldn't bear the feel of their icy touch on my skin. I raised both hands to the sides of my face, trying to keep their hands away.

To my surprise, their angry mumbles and murmurs faded. The room grew silent.

Slowly, I opened my eyes. I blinked a few times. Bright light shone down from above.

A face loomed over me. Mr. Piccolo. His eyeglasses gleamed in the light. He leaned over me, his face tight with concern.

"Kate? Are you okay? How do you feel?"

"I . . ." My throat felt too dry to speak. It took me a while to realize I was on my back. On the floor. He was on his knees, leaning over me. "Where . . . ?" I choked out.

"You and Courtney had a bad fall," he said, studying my face. "You've been out cold for a minute or two. We were all very worried."

I raised my head off the floor. "Ow." A hard, throbbing headache made me lie back down.

Over Mr. P's shoulder, I saw other kids huddled against the wall, watching tensely. And I saw Paco near the door, hands shoved in his jeans pockets.

Paco. He wasn't a ghost. I mean, he *isn't* a ghost.

I was dreaming. That whole frightening scene with Paco and the ghosts was a crazy dream while I was knocked unconscious.

Mr. P's bald head glowed under the ceiling lights. He frowned at me. "Do you feel strong enough to sit up?"

"I . . . think so," I said.

He grabbed my shoulders and helped me into a sitting position. "Okay?"

"Okay," I said. I was still trying to force that ghost scene from my mind.

"No broken bones?" Mr. P asked.

I tested my arms, my legs. "I think I'm okay."

"That trapdoor shouldn't have been open," he said, shaking his head. "Luckily, you didn't fall very far."

"How *is* Courtney?" I asked.

She appeared beside Mr. P. Her white wig was disheveled and some of the white ghost makeup had smeared off her cheeks. "I'm okay," she said. "Luckily, I landed on top of you. Thanks for breaking my fall."

Chalk up another win for Courtney.

"Any time," I said.

I was starting to feel better. I climbed to my knees, then stood up. "Where are we?"

"In the basement under the stage," Mr. P said. "Let's go back upstairs, people."

He wiped sweat off his forehead with a handkerchief. I could see he was very relieved that Courtney and I weren't hurt.

He motioned for the others to follow the hall to the stairs. But he held Courtney and me back. Courtney tried to fix her hair. I knew I must look a mess, but I didn't care. I had no broken bones, and there weren't any ugly ghosts forcing me to sing.

"I'm very disappointed in both of you," Mr. P said, mopping his forehead some more. "Disappointed and surprised."

"It was her fault —" Courtney started. But Mr. P raised a hand to cut her off.

"That was the kind of fighting that could get you girls suspended from school," he said. "I'm not going to do that. But I'm not giving you the part you want in the Christmas play, either."

We both stared at him. "You mean —" I started.

"I mean I've given the part of Livvy, the lead sister, to Carol Ann."

"No way!" Courtney cried.

I remained silent. My brain was spinning around. I was glad Courtney didn't get the part. But I felt bad that I had totally lost it, totally lost my temper and acted like a wild animal.

"You two can be in the chorus," Mr. P said. "If you promise to get along and not start any more fights."

She and I mumbled okay. He stared at us till we shook hands.

As soon as he was out of the room, Courtney turned to me, her eyes blazing angrily. "This is all your fault. You ruined it for both of us."

"My fault? I didn't lock *you* in Mr. P's office," I snapped. I had a strong urge to grab her by the neck and shake her till her head fell off.

Uh-oh. *Kate, get control.*

But how could I not hate Courtney?

As soon as she saw Jack upstairs in the auditorium, she started to limp. As if she'd hurt herself in the fall.

He hurried over to help her walk down the aisle.

Watching her lean on him, another wave of anger swept over me.

Courtney knows I like Jack. She's faking that limp to get his attention.

Okay, okay. It was a bad night.

I wasn't going to have a starring role. I was only going to be in the chorus.

I could handle that. And I guess now I'd have the time to deal with my other problems.

Namely, how could I get the kids to stop teasing me and calling me Ghost Girl? And, how could I stop Courtney from ruining my life?

Of course, I didn't realize that I had much bigger problems ahead. I had no way of knowing that I was about to enter a haunted world — and might never see the school, my parents, or my friends again.

PART TWO

TWELVE SCREAMS

20

The day after the tryouts, Mr. Piccolo said he didn't want to rehearse the play in the school auditorium. He said he wanted to take us away for the weekend to a place where we'd really feel the right atmosphere.

He said he was taking us to an old house in the next town, on a street called Ardmore Road. I'd never heard of it. He said the house was right across the street from a graveyard. It was dark and creepy and had been empty for years. The perfect place to get in the right mood and rehearse his Christmas play.

So, three days later, I sat between Carol Ann and Paco in the back of the school bus. Outside, the morning sun was still a red ball just climbing over the tops of the trees. A hard rain the night before had melted all the snow, except for a few ugly patches along the side of the road.

Kids screamed as the bus hit a sharp bump. I nearly bounced into Paco's lap.

A big red-haired dude named Shawn O'Hara pretended to fall into the aisle. Shawn is a real clown. He is always falling off his chair or walking into walls. He once told Mrs. Wentz that when he grows up, he wants to be a cartoon character.

I think he was serious.

Up near the front of the bus, I saw Courtney sitting next to Jack. She was pretending to slap him. She tickled him, and shoved him toward the window. Totally flirting with him, and he was really into it.

Courtney had been flirting with Jack ever since the tryouts three nights ago. And I knew she didn't really care that much about him. She just wanted to make sure I saw her claim another victory.

I told myself I was going to ignore her all weekend. Sure, we'd be staying in an old house together, and we'd be singing together in the chorus. But I vowed I wouldn't let anything she said or did annoy me.

No way I was going to lose it this weekend.

Carol Ann looked awesome. She's totally the hottest-looking girl in our class. And the nicest. She had her silky blond hair tied behind her head in a tight ponytail. Under her down parka, she wore a cowl-necked blue ski sweater that matched her eyes. And she had a short black skirt over black tights, and black Ugg boots.

She and Paco were leaning across me, arguing about Pop-Tarts. Carol Ann said they were too sweet for breakfast. Paco insisted you need the sugar in the morning for energy.

"Let's say you have a couple of Pop-Tarts without icing," he said. "Well, then you drag around all morning because you didn't get enough sugar."

"You can put sugar in a bowl of cereal," Carol Ann told him. "Or have Frosted Flakes or something."

"Cereal takes too long to eat," Paco said. "I'm always late. I just grab some Pop-Tarts and wolf them down on the way to school. I don't even toast them."

"Gross," I said. "Do you eat them still in the wrapper?"

"No. I take them out first," Paco said. He's a little lame in the sense-of-humor department.

"Did you know my mom is a nutritionist?" I said.

Paco squinted at me. "Does that mean you have to eat vegetables?"

I laughed. "Sometimes."

He shook his head. "Now *that's* gross."

The bus squealed as it made a sharp turn. I read the street sign out the window: N ARDMORE ROAD.

"This is the street," I said. "We must be almost there."

"Do you think they'll have Pop-Tarts?" Paco asked, grinning.

"Could you shut up about Pop-Tarts?" Carol Ann said.

"No, I can't."

"The house we're staying in is supposed to be old and run-down and spooky," I said, trying to change the subject.

"Perfect," Carol Ann said. "We'll feel like we're living inside Mr. P's play."

"That's the idea," I said.

As I said, the play is about a family that spends Christmas in a haunted house. The ghosts of the house terrify the family. There are lots of thrills and chills. Twelve horrifying screams. Terrible things happen. But in the end, they celebrate Christmas together and learn that the holiday is meant for everyone.

There are a lot of songs. But it's a pretty scary Christmas play. And Mr. P said he knew we'd do a better job with it if we rehearsed in a really scary place.

We all were bounced forward as the bus squealed to a sudden stop. "Here we go!" the driver called. "Everybody out."

I squinted out the dust-smeared window. I could see a tall iron fence stretching down the block. Behind the fence, I saw rows of gravestones. Patches of snow between the graves. The cemetery.

The back of my neck tingled. I didn't like being so close to a graveyard. But I had no choice.

I turned and gazed out the window across the aisle. Past a small, square front yard, a tall gray house filled the bus window. I could see a broken awning over a wide front stoop and black shutters tilting at dark windows.

Up front, Courtney turned to me. "See any ghosts yet, Ghost Girl?"

Some kids laughed. I just ignored her.

I followed Paco and Carol Ann out of the bus. Just as we stepped onto the ground, the sun slid behind clouds. The sky faded to a deep gray, making the old house appear even more dark and frightening.

"Welcome to the haunted house!" a voice called. "Give up all hope, ye who enter here." Mr. P stepped out of the house, onto the front stoop, his arms spread in welcome. He wore a long black overcoat. His head was topped with a Santa hat, tilted to one side.

"How did you turn off the sun?" Shawn shouted.

"It's all special effects," Mr. P said. "I hope this old place creeps you out and gets you in the mood."

The driver started to pull our bags from the compartment in the side of the bus. "Your rooms are ready," Mr. P said. "It's cold in the house, but I started a fire. That should warm things up."

The air felt cold. The sun stayed hidden behind a wall of clouds. I pulled my hood up and zipped my parka to the top. Then I picked up the canvas bag my mom had helped me pack and carried it to the house.

A steep stairway stood in front of the narrow entryway. To the left, I could see the flickering light of the fire in the front room. I shivered. The air felt colder inside the house than outside.

Carol Ann rubbed her nose. "We're going to freeze," she said. "Look. I can see my breath."

Mr. P appeared behind us. "I'm working on starting up the furnace," he said, rubbing his hands, trying to warm them. "It hasn't been used in a long time. But we'll get the house nice and toasty."

He led the way up the steep stairs. The old floorboards creaked and groaned. The wood banister was loose and wobbled from side to side as I slid my hand along it.

"Careful," Mr. P warned. "Some of the stairs are rotting. Hold on to the banister."

"But the banister is loose," I called.

He turned, a frown on his face. "This house is more dangerous than I remembered."

Remembered?

"Mr. P, have you been here before?" Jack asked.

Mr. P didn't answer. Maybe he didn't hear him.

The bedrooms were along a twisting, dimly lit hall on the second floor. The wallpaper was torn and peeling. Dark paintings covered the walls, so dark I couldn't see what was on them. A tall vase of wilted, dead flowers stood on a table against the wall.

Mr. P assigned Courtney, Carol Ann, and me the first bedroom. It was a big square room with a furry carpet on the floor. Three cots had been placed against the walls.

Of course, Courtney instantly claimed the cot farthest from the window. I got the window cot. I could feel the cold air leaking through the rattling window frame. I was glad Mom forced me to pack my woolly nightshirt.

Carol Ann shivered. She pointed out the window. "We're facing the backyard. Look. There is an old shack out there and a big garden shed. And an old-fashioned well."

"I can't wait to explore the place," I said.

Courtney claimed the top dresser drawer and began to shove her stuff into it. "Kate, see any ghosts yet?" she asked.

"Courtney, isn't that getting a little stale?" I said. "Why don't we declare a truce?"

"Yes. Why don't we?" she said. Then she laughed and shook her head. "Whatever."

I decided I'd unpack later. Carol Ann and I hurried downstairs.

Mr. P greeted us in the front room. He was standing close to the fire in the wide fireplace, warming his hands. He had taken off his overcoat. But he still had the Santa hat tilted on his head.

"People, why don't you take some time to explore the house and the backyard?" he said. "I think you'll find it very interesting. We'll start our rehearsals after lunch."

I saw Jack and Shawn wander down the hall toward the kitchen. Some other kids followed them. I decided to explore the backyard instead.

Carol Ann followed me through a side door and around to the back. The sun had come out, but the sky was still a pale gray. Shadows from the tall trees in the yard appeared to crawl over the ground, which was bare except for clumps of low weeds.

We gazed at the small guesthouse. Part of the roof had collapsed and tilted against the side of the house. The shack and the shed stood side-by-side, paint peeling. A bare tree branch lay on the ground beneath the fat old tree it had fallen from.

"I'm trying to picture what this looked like back in the day," Carol Ann said. "I mean, when everything was fresh and new."

I turned and saw Courtney coming around the side of the house. "Let's keep walking," I said. "I don't want her to catch up."

Carol Ann scrunched up her face. "What's up with you and Courtney? What's her problem?"

I shrugged. "Who knows?"

Our shoes crunched over the hard ground. Carol Ann walked up to one of the sheds and tugged open the door. She screamed as a dozen mice came scurrying out.

I laughed. "It's only mice!"

"But I wasn't expecting a stampede," she said.

I kept walking toward the back fence. I had my eye on the old-fashioned stone well in front of me. It had a little pointed roof above it.

I took out my phone and snapped a photo of it.

I suddenly felt drawn to the well, as if it was pulling me toward it.

Why did I have this strange feeling about it?

My skin began to tingle. My legs felt heavy. A feeling of dread swept over me.

Why? Why was I frightened of this old well? Part of me wanted to back away. Get as far from the well as I could.

But part of me felt a force pulling me closer to examine it.

I stepped up to the well and grabbed the top with both hands. Some of the stones had crumbled off. A section of the wall across from me had broken. There were no stones on the ground. They had probably fallen into the well.

I leaned against the stone wall. The stones were cold and powdery.

Is there still water at the bottom?

My whole body tingled. I had such a weird feeling about this well. Something was wrong here, terribly wrong.

But I couldn't pull back. I couldn't resist.

I had to see what was at the bottom.

I leaned over the wall and peered down.

I heard the crumbling sound beneath me. Too late. Too late.

The wall gave way. It fell apart and I toppled forward.

I let out a shrill scream as I started to fall headfirst down the well.

21

I shot my hands out — and grabbed nothing but air.

As I fell, my legs scraped over the stone wall. Then my shoes caught on the edge.

With a breathless cry, I swung out my arms again and grabbed the side of the well. Then I flipped myself up, hoisted myself out, and somehow landed on my feet.

Not my best landing.

But how lucky that I'd been a gymnast. It saved my life.

I stood there for a long time, feeling shaky, trying to catch my breath. I kept picturing the stone walls stretching down . . . down . . . to nothing but darkness. A black pit.

Carol Ann came running over. Courtney stood watching from the side of the little guesthouse.

"Kate? Are you okay?" Carol Ann cried. "I . . . I saw you fall and —"

"Yeah. I'm just a little shaken," I said. "I mean, I can't stop shaking. I almost —"

"You almost gave me a heart attack," Carol Ann said. She rushed forward and hugged me. "I really thought you fell down the well."

I gazed back at the well. The top was all ragged because of the stones that had crumbled off. I shuddered again.

"Why did you lean over like that?" Carol Ann demanded.

I blinked. "I . . . don't know," I said. "Something weird happened. The well seemed to pull me . . ."

"Let's go inside now." Mr. P suddenly appeared. He was dressed in black sweats. He had taken off the Santa cap.

Had he seen me fall?

"I forgot to warn everyone to stay away from the old well," he said, leading the way back to the house. "It's dangerous."

Tell me about it.

We started to the house. Courtney was waiting by the garden shed. "See anything down in that well?" she asked.

"Too dark," I said. "It's really deep. I couldn't see the bottom."

She nodded and turned away.

Mr. P ushered everyone into the front room. The fire in the fireplace crackled and danced. We all perched on the old couches and chairs and drank hot mulled cider from mugs.

Mr. P stood in front of the fireplace, waiting for us to get quiet. "I'll tell you the story of this house," he said, setting down his mug of cider. "It's a sad story. And you will soon see that it is the inspiration for my Christmas play."

His eyeglasses reflected the orange and yellow flames from the fire behind him. He pulled up a low wooden stool and settled down to tell his story.

"There are tales and rumors that this house is haunted," he started. "That's the reason no one has lived here in a long, long time. Over a hundred years ago, a family moved in. A mother, father, two twin boys named Ned and Abe, and a little girl named Flora."

He picked up the cider mug and took a sip. "The family had just moved in," he said. "It was Christmastime — and tragedy struck. The story goes that Flora, the eight-year-old girl, fell into the well. The twins saw her fall. They heard her screams as she tried to stay afloat at the bottom. The parents came running. But they were helpless. They had no way to save her."

Mr. P rolled the cider mug between his hands. "Flora pleaded for her family to do something to get her out. She screamed, 'Get me out!' twelve times. Then she went silent. When the family peered down to the bottom of the well, all they could see was her red cap floating on the water. Flora was gone.

"The story goes that the family has haunted this house ever since. They appear only at Christmastime. Waiting . . . waiting for someone to bring the little girl back so they can celebrate the holiday as they used to."

A hush fell over the room. The only sound was the crackle and pop of the fire.

Shawn broke the silence. "Mr. P, are you making this all up?" he asked.

Mr. P shook his head. He raised his right hand, as if swearing. "It's a true story, Shawn," he said. "It's been handed down in my family for generations. You see, that family . . . those people who lived in this house were my ancestors. Probably my great-great-great-great grandparents."

"So that's where you got the idea for the play?" Paco asked.

Mr. P nodded. "Yes. But of course, I gave it a happy ending because it's a Christmas play. I figured out a way to bring Flora up from the well and make everyone have a happy Christmas."

"So is this house really haunted?" Jack asked. "Did you really bring us all to a haunted house where angry ghosts live?"

"It's almost Christmas. When do the ghosts come out?" Shawn said.

Mr. P snickered. "Do you guys seriously believe in ghosts?"

"Kate does," Courtney chimed in. "Kate sees ghosts everywhere. She's probably watching some ghosts right now."

"Shut up," I said. The words just slipped out. I wanted to bite my tongue. I promised myself I wouldn't get into any fights with Courtney.

Courtney made an ugly face at me.

Mr. P ignored us both. "No. I don't believe in ghosts, people," he said. "I think maybe the story of the girl falling down the well is true. But I don't believe that the ghost family still lives here and appears every Christmas. That's just a story someone made up a long time ago."

Shawn did a ghost howl. "Owooooooooo."

A few other kids took up the howl.

Mr. P motioned for them to stop.

Kids laughed. Shawn jumped to his feet and made his whole body shake. "Ooh, I'm scared. I'm scared."

"I hope you all won't be disappointed," Mr. P said. "But you won't see any ghosts here this weekend. I wouldn't bring you to a dangerous haunted house just to get you in the right mood to perform in my play — *would* I?"

No one answered that question.

I gazed around. The fire sent long, flickering shadows over the room. Through the front window, I could see the afternoon sun lowering itself behind the trees.

Mr. P hoisted himself up from the low stool. He tugged his big sweatshirt down over his belly and clapped his hands together. "Time to get to work, people. I want to rehearse the play from the opening song." He glanced from face to face. "How many of you have memorized your parts?"

Courtney was the first to raise her hand. A few other kids raised hands, too.

"Well, I need you to memorize, memorize, memorize," Mr. P said. "By the end of the weekend, I don't want anyone using their scripts."

He lined everyone up in front of the fire. To start the play, all the actors had to stand in a line and sing the "12 Screams of Christmas" song. The four kids in the chorus are off to the side. We sing, too.

I took my place between Courtney and a boy named DeCarlos. DeCarlos is tall and lanky, with dark skin, big brown eyes, and an awesome, friendly smile.

He's the best singer of all of us. But he's totally shy, and when he tried out for the father role, he mumbled the words and no one could hear him. So Mr. P put him in the chorus.

"Crisp, people," Mr. P shouted. "That's the word of the day. When you sing the song, think *crisp*. Sing the words crisply. Keep the tempo up. Okay. Let's try it all the way through."

He gave a signal, and we all began to sing.

"On the first day of Christmas, my true love screamed, 'I see . . .
A buzzard in a bare tree.'
On the second day of Christmas, my true love screamed, 'I see . . .
Two haunted houses
And a buzzard in a bare tree.'
On the third day of Christmas, my true love screamed, 'I see . . .
Three ghostly spirits,
Two haunted houses,
And a buzzard in a bare tree.'"

It sounded pretty good. Our voices rang off the high ceiling of the room.

But I had one problem. Courtney kept elbowing me. She stood in front of me and sang at the top of her lungs, drowning me out. And drowning out the other two chorus members, too.

DeCarlos flashed me a smile. He and I both knew there was nothing we could do about Courtney. She was acting like she was the star of the show.

That was one problem. But then I had another one. A frightening one.

Because as we sang the opening song, my eyes went to the stairway just beyond the front room. And perched on the banister, I saw two boys. Two dark-haired boys.

I squinted hard and realized they were twins.

Twins dressed in ragged shirts and torn overalls. They leaned on the banister and watched us sing.

I poked DeCarlos and motioned to the stairs with my eyes.

He turned, gazed at the stairway, and shrugged.

"See them?" I whispered.

He looked again. "See what?"

On the stairway, one boy scratched his dark hair. The other boy leaned on the banister, staring at us intently.

And I knew Mr. P was wrong about this house.

I knew I was staring at two ghosts. The ghosts of the boys in his story.

22

*"On the fourth day of Christmas, my true love
screamed, 'I see . . .
Four devil bats,
Three ghostly spirits,
Two haunted houses,
And a buzzard in a bare tree.'"*

The song continued. I wanted to scream. I
wanted to point to the stairs. I wanted to warn
everyone there were ghosts in the room.

But with Courtney pressed right beside me,
singing her heart out, somehow I held the scream
in. I forced myself to stay quiet. No way I wanted
to give her another chance to embarrass me in
front of everyone.

I didn't scream. I held it in till my chest felt
about to burst. I glanced up and saw Mr. P staring at me. He must have guessed something
was wrong.

He waved both hands above his head and stopped the singing. "Kate, are you okay?" he called.

Everyone turned to look at me. Courtney took a step back and studied me.

I watched the boys on the stairs. One of them whispered something to the other.

"Don't you see them? Don't you see the twin boys?"

That's what I was desperate to say. But I knew no one else saw them. I knew I had to keep quiet about them.

"I'm . . . okay," I told Mr. P.

"You stopped singing, so I thought maybe there was a problem," he said.

There IS a problem. This house is haunted.

"No problem," I said. "I just lost my place. Sorry."

"Let's start again from the beginning," Mr. P said. "And people, remember, I want it *crisp*."

We started the song again. I forced a smile to my face and tried to pretend nothing was wrong. I could see Mr. P watching me as we sang.

I tried to duck behind Courtney. I wanted to keep my eyes on the twin boys on the steps.

When the song ended, kids scattered around the room.

"Places for scene one," Mr. P called. "No break time. Take your places, people."

The chorus wasn't in scene one. Courtney started to say something to me. But I pushed past her, darted through a clump of kids in the center of the room, and strode toward the stairs.

Would the two boys turn and run?

No.

They stared at me as I came toward them. Now I could clearly see their pale faces, skin peeling off their cheeks and foreheads, their dark, glassy, dead eyes.

Their long-sleeved shirts had once been white. But now they were gray with splotches of brown, the buttons missing on the front, and ragged holes in the sleeves. Their overalls were stained, torn at the knees.

They stared at me and didn't move. Their faces were hard, their expressions cold. They studied me with those round, dark eyes, as if they didn't believe I could see them.

"Hey," I said. I didn't know what to say.

And suddenly, I wondered what I was doing. Why was I approaching these two dead boys? How could I just step up to a ghost?

A shock of fear made my whole body shudder. *They've been dead for over a hundred years. You can't just walk up and say hi.*

I froze a few feet from the staircase.

They shifted their weight and slid their hands along the wooden banister. They kept their eyes on me, as if giving me the evil eye.

The evil eye.

A staring match. I stood there shaking, not believing I could see them so closely. Not believing I could stand so close to two ghosts from long ago.

And then one of them spoke in a harsh whisper. *"We'll be back, Flora."*

I gasped. Did I hear him right?

"I . . . I'm not Flora," I stammered.

He and his brother vanished. Disappeared before my eyes.

But the whisper lingered: *"We'll be back."*

23

After dinner, Carol Ann, Courtney, and I were upstairs in our room. The wind rattled the window above my cot, and I felt gusts of cold air as I sat and gazed down on the backyard.

I'll have to sleep with my sweatshirt over my nightshirt. Otherwise, I'll freeze.

Across the room, Courtney was sprawled on her back on her cot, texting someone on her phone. Carol Ann sat on the edge of her cot with the script in her hands, mouthing the words, trying to memorize her lines.

"Mr. P changed the old ghost story a lot," she said. "For one thing, there are *three* sisters in the play. Not just Flora. Flora is the youngest of the three now. And the twin boys. I asked him why, and he said he wanted to make parts for more kids."

"Oh," I said. I wasn't really listening. I had my back to her as I peered out at the night. A shiny half-moon hung low in the purple sky. A strong, steady wind sent dead leaves scuttling across the grass.

I was dying to tell Carol Ann about the twin boys I saw. But not with Courtney in the room. No way. Carol Ann probably wouldn't believe me. But she wouldn't tease and torture me about it.

"I wish the chorus had more to do," Courtney said. "We only have three songs. How boring is that?"

"At least you don't have to learn pages and pages of lines," Carol Ann said. "I'm playing Livvy, and Livvy never shuts up! She just keeps talking and talking."

Courtney said something, but I didn't hear it. I was concentrating on sounds I heard. They seemed to be coming from the yard below. Voices? Whispers?

I leaned into the drafty window and struggled to hear.

A few hours later, Carol Ann was asleep on her back with the open script resting on her stomach. She fell asleep while still trying to memorize her part.

Courtney was asleep on her side. Snoring softly, she had the covers pulled up over her head.

I couldn't sleep. My brain was whirring. I was alert to every sound. Every groan the old house made. Every creak of a floorboard.

This house is haunted. The ghosts could come into our room at any time.

How could I sleep in a haunted house? How could I relax at all, knowing that I was the only one who could see them?

I sat up on my cot and gazed out the window. I tugged my sweatshirt tight. The cold seeped in from outside.

The half-moon was high in the sky now. It sent a pale light over the entire yard. All was still. The wind had stopped.

I stared down at the little guesthouse. Silent and dark.

The old well at the back of the yard caught my eye. The moonlight appeared to make the stone wall shine.

I shuddered, remembering my close call that afternoon. How I nearly plunged headfirst to the bottom.

I hugged myself, partly from the cold, partly from my frightening thoughts.

I stared at the old stone well. And I felt the pull again. Something drawing me to that well. Something urging me to go out there.

Something very strange. Just a feeling. A strong urge to stand up and sneak down the stairs and out the back door.

Go out to the well. You must go to the well.

And as I sat on the cot, hugging myself tightly, gazing down, feeling the strong pull of the well . . . like gravity . . . as I sat hunched there, I suddenly heard a whispered voice.

A soft whisper. But so clear ... so perfectly clear ...

"Help me. Please ... help me. Please ... help me."

Struggling to catch my breath, I jumped to my feet and scrambled into my clothes.

24

I couldn't find my parka in the dark. And I didn't want to turn on the light and wake Courtney and Carol Ann.

So I headed outside in my sweatshirt and jeans. Dim lights had been left on in the front room and the hall that led to the kitchen. I tried to walk on tiptoe. But the old floorboards still creaked under my shoes.

I struggled with the lock on the kitchen door, pulled it open, and stepped into the backyard.

The ground was crunchy and hard as I started to walk toward the well. The tall grass was wet from the night dew.

A scrawny rabbit stood tall on its hind legs in front of the garden shed. It stood frozen, still as a statue, dark eyes watching me. As I crunched toward it, the creature spun and took off, disappearing behind the shed.

The air felt cold against my hot face. It carried

the sweet smell of fireplace smoke. Some house had a fire going nearby. I took a deep breath. I raised my eyes to the low wall that zigzagged through the yard. Then to the well at the back fence.

"Oh." I uttered a soft cry as I heard the whispers again.

"Help me ... Please ... help me."

A cold shiver ran down my whole body.

A gust of icy wind blew my hair over my eyes. I brushed it back and gazed around.

Where were the whispers coming from?

My eyes stopped at the well.

I didn't want to go back there. That well already meant nothing but horror to me.

"Help me ... Please...."

I couldn't stop shivering. Not from the cold. From that sad whispered voice, so tiny, so far away and nearby at the same time.

Mr. P's story raced through my mind. The little girl. Flora. Down in the well. Screaming for help twelve times. Then ... silence.

That was just a ghost story handed down by his family. Mr. P said he didn't believe the story. He didn't believe in ghosts.

But now I felt that strange, frightening pull again, forcing me to move, drawing me to the well. And again, I heard the frantic whisper:

"Help ... Help ... Help me...."

"This is crazy," I murmured out loud. "This can't be happening."

Someone is playing a joke on you, Kate.

I spun back to the house. Was it Courtney? Had Courtney whispered up in the bedroom? Had she followed me out here to the backyard?

No sign of her. It was her kind of joke. But she wasn't here. She was asleep upstairs.

I was alone in the yard. Alone and shivering. And listening to the whispers.

"Help me . . . Help me . . . Please . . . help me."

And now my legs were moving, almost without my control. My legs were carrying me to the old well. My shoes crunched the ground. I hugged myself tightly, trying to stop the shivers.

I couldn't stop my legs. I couldn't turn or head in another direction. Something was pulling me . . . against my will.

And then there I was, standing at the side of the well. The stones reflecting the pale yellow moonlight.

The wind had stopped.

The whispers had stopped.

Silence now.

Total silence.

My breath came out in a shuddering puff. I could see it steam up in front of me.

I grabbed the top of the wall. Grabbed it

tightly with both hands. The stones felt cold to my touch, colder than the air.

I have no choice. It won't let go of me. I have to look.

Grasping the wall, I leaned forward — and peered down into the well.

25

A slant of moonlight lit the wall across from me. I could see the smooth stones clearly. But the light stopped two-thirds of the way down. Below stretched only a heavy blackness.

I gripped the cold stones at the top. I tested them with my hands as I leaned over the edge. Tested them to make sure they weren't about to break off and send me plunging down again.

I stared down at the dark, round bottom. I could hear the faint splash of water down there.

I took a deep breath and shouted: "Anyone down there?"

My voice echoed all the way down.

No reply. Silence.

Of COURSE there was no reply.

Was I losing my mind?

I pushed back. I wanted to get away from there. I wanted to get back to my room and under the warm covers.

But as I started to stand up, something caught my eye.

A flash of color. In the black bottom of the well.

I grasped the top of the wall and peered down again. The moonlight had shifted. And in its pale glow, I saw something floating on the dark water.

A flash of red. I squinted hard. A red cap.

"No!" The cry burst from my throat.

I pushed myself up. Forced myself to stand up straight and spin away from the well.

No. Impossible, Kate. Impossible.

You didn't see that.

I had to move. I had to run. Run back to the house.

But before I could move, hands grabbed my arms. Hands grasped me roughly on both sides and held me in place.

"Hey!" I screamed. "You —"

My scream cut off as I stared into the milk-white faces and glowing black eyes of the dark-haired twin brothers.

26

"L-let go," I stammered.

The moonlight reflected off their dark, glassy eyes. Their faces were identical. Their expression hard. They held my arms with surprising strength.

They wore the same ragged shirts and pants as that afternoon. Their hair rustled in the steady breeze.

"Who are you?" I cried. "What do you want?" My voice came out shrill, frightened.

"Come with us," one of them said. He looked to be eleven or twelve, but he had a little boy's soft voice.

"Come home with us," his twin said.

"No. Let go." I squirmed and twisted.

They held on tight.

"Are you . . . ghosts?" I blurted out. In my fear, I couldn't think straight. I didn't know what I was saying.

"I'm Ned," the one on my left said. "He's Abe."

"What do you want?" I cried. "Why won't you let me go?"

"Come home for Christmas," Ned said.

"We need you home for Christmas," Abe echoed. "You'll be Flora."

"Huh? Flora?" My breath caught in my throat. "I'm not Flora!" I cried. "I'm Kate."

"You'll be Flora," Ned insisted, narrowing his eyes at me. In the white moonlight, his eyes appeared sunken, blank. His mouth was set in a hard frown. He suddenly looked menacing. They both did.

I felt a shudder of fear.

Their hands were so hard on my arm. So bony and cold. Hands of the dead.

"Are you ghosts? What are you doing? Where are you taking me?" The questions gushed from my mouth like a waterfall.

"We live here," Ned said, pointing to the house. "We have always lived here, haven't we, Abe?"

"Always," Abe said.

They tugged me toward the house. I tried to pull back, but they were too strong. Too strong for normal twelve-year-olds.

"Now you will live with us, Flora," Abe said.

I gasped. "No. Don't you see? I'm not Flora."

"You shall be Flora," Abe replied in a cold, flat voice. "You shall be Flora for Christmas."

"And forever," Ned added.

"Excuse me?" I cried. "What did you just say?"

"Flora, you will stay with us forever," Ned repeated.

They tugged me past the guesthouse, past the garden shed.

"I'm not Flora," I said again. "Listen to me. I'm Kate. My name is Kate. And I live in Brooks Village. The next town. I don't live here."

Abe turned to me. His face kept shimmering in and out of focus. Light, then dark. Light, then dark. "Don't fight, Flora," he whispered.

"You always like to fight with us," Ned said. "Since you were a little baby."

"You have so much wild spirit," his twin added. "You like to tease us and mimic us and follow us and act up with us. But now it is Christmas, Flora. And you are home. Pa says Christmas is the time to enjoy each other, to celebrate each other."

"Ma and Pa will be so glad to see you," Ned said. "We have missed you for so many years. And waited for your return. This will be the best Christmas in history."

"WHY DON'T YOU LISTEN TO ME?" I screamed.

Both boys didn't react at all.

"You know how much you enjoy singing all the carols," Abe said.

"And lighting the candles on the Christmas tree," Ned added.

The house loomed in front of us. "Where are

you taking me?" I demanded. "Can't you see that I'm not Flora?"

They stopped pulling me. Ned loosened his grip on my arm. "My brother and I know that you aren't Flora," he said, his face hidden in shadow. All I could see was the dull glow of his dead eyes. "We know you are not our sister."

"But we have waited so long," Abe said. "And now it's Christmas, and we need Flora back. So . . . you are our choice."

"You will be Flora now . . . forever," his twin said.

I swallowed hard. "Forever? What do you mean?"

"Ghosts are immortal, Flora," Abe said.

"Ghosts live forever," Ned said in a dreamy whisper. "You will like it, Flora."

"But . . . But . . ." I sputtered.

They forced me toward the kitchen door.

"But . . . don't I have to *die* to be a ghost?" I cried.

They both nodded. They raised their cold eyes to me. I felt my body shudder again.

"It won't take long," Ned said in a whisper.

27

"No!"

I uttered a sharp cry. I dropped back and slid my arms free.

The boys spun in surprise.

I did a backflip. Landed on my feet. Turned to run.

But they were beside me quickly. They clamped their hard fingers around my elbows and held me in place.

"There's nowhere to run, Flora," Ned said softly, in a low, flat voice.

"You can't escape," his twin whispered. "You want to come home for the holidays, don't you?"

"No!" I screamed. "Please — let me go!"

They didn't reply. They turned me around and began to pull me to the kitchen door again.

"We'll sing all your favorite carols," Abe said. "And we'll all sit down to Christmas dinner."

"It's been waiting on the table for over one hundred years," Ned said. "All of your favorites."

"No. Please. You know I'm not Flora. Please —
stop this," I cried.

And then the kitchen door swung open. I let
out a cry of surprise as Mr. P burst out. He wore
a long bathrobe that came down nearly to his
bare feet. Behind his glasses, his eyes darted
from side to side over the backyard until he spotted me.

"Kate? What on earth. What are you doing
out here this time of night?"

*Don't you see them? Don't you see the two boys
gripping my arms, pulling me to the house?*

I could still see Ned and Abe. I could still feel
their tight grip on my arms. They had turned to
Mr. P, their pale faces open in surprise.

"I . . . I . . ." I stammered.

I wanted to scream: "They're holding me.
They're dragging me to their Christmas
celebration."

But Mr. P had his eyes on me. Only on me. He
couldn't see them. And if I told him what was
happening, he would think I was totally losing it.
He would just think I was crazy.

"I . . . needed some fresh air," I said.

He frowned at me, fiddling with the belt to his
bathrobe. "It's too cold out here, Kate. Courtney
and Carol Ann were worried about you. They
said they couldn't find you."

"I couldn't sleep," I said. "Too excited about
everything, I guess."

Mr. P took a step toward me, and the boys' hands slid off my arms. They vanished in a puff of cold air. The last thing I saw was their dark eyes. Their faces were gone, but the eyes lingered, like glowing, dark coals. Then they vanished, too.

I stumbled forward, startled that the twins had let me go. I heard soft whispers on the wind: *"Flora ... Flora ..."*

The sound made me shiver.

Mr. P motioned to the door. "Come inside. Hurry. Look at you. You're shivering. What's wrong with you, Kate? You're not even wearing a coat."

"I just ... needed air," I repeated. It sounded so lame.

I followed him into the kitchen. He closed the door behind us. He flashed on the ceiling light. "I'll make us both some hot tea to warm up," he said.

I dropped down at the kitchen counter, hugging myself, trying to stop my teeth from chattering.

"Why didn't you tell Courtney and Carol Ann where you were going?" Mr. P asked, putting the kettle on the stove.

"They were asleep," I said. "I only planned to go outside for a minute."

He opened a cabinet and pulled down a box of tea bags. Then he found two white mugs in the next cabinet.

"I know you and Courtney have issues. . . ." he said.

I shut my eyes. I raised both hands and tried to rub the cold off my cheeks.

I have to tell him about the ghost twins, I told myself.

I have to tell him he has brought us to a haunted house. I have to let him know that we are in danger.

I can't keep it from him. I have to tell him they called me Flora and said they were going to turn me into a ghost.

Can I make him believe me?

Can I make him believe that I'm not crazy? That I'm telling the frightening truth?

I still had my eyes shut. I pressed both palms against my cheeks. I couldn't get them warm.

I took a deep breath. "Mr. P," I started. "I have to tell you something. Please don't think I'm crazy. Please believe me. But that story you told us about the family that lived here, and the little girl who fell in the well? It's true. And they're still here. I saw the two brothers. Abe and Ned. They grabbed me outside. They were pulling me to the house when you showed up."

I opened my eyes. "Mr. P? Do you believe me? Please. I'm not crazy. Do you believe me?"

28

I blinked. And gazed around the kitchen.

He wasn't there. He had left the room. He hadn't heard a word I said.

With a sigh, I sank lower on the tall stool, placed my elbows on the counter, and covered my face again. I didn't move until the kettle began to whistle. Then I jumped off the stool and began to pour the boiling water into the two mugs.

Mr. P strode back into the kitchen. "Sorry," he said. "I went upstairs to tell Courtney and Carol Ann you were okay. But they had gone back to sleep."

"Guess they weren't too worried about me," I said. I peered out the kitchen window. Under the silvery moonlight, I could see the well at the back of the yard.

I shivered and turned away from it.

Maybe I'll tell Mr. P tomorrow, I decided. *Maybe tomorrow, I'll think of a way to make him believe me....*

The next morning, Mr. P had us all in the front room to rehearse the beginning to Act Two. The act opened with a song, so the chorus members were included.

I'd had about three hours sleep, and I was feeling groggy and totally out of it. I kept forcing back yawn after yawn.

I couldn't do anything with my hair. So I borrowed a red-and-blue Cubs cap from Carol Ann and pulled it down on my head. I'd put on some blush and pink lip gloss to make me look almost alive. Not sure it helped.

Believe me, I was not in the mood for Courtney's sarcasm. But I had plenty of it at breakfast. She accused me of going on a ghost hunt in the middle of the night. And she got a big laugh by saying that I looked so scary this morning, I frightened all the ghosts out of this haunted house.

Ha-ha.

I tried to ignore her, but it wasn't easy. I wanted to scream, *"There really ARE ghosts here. I've SEEN them. Maybe they'd like to take YOU to their Christmas dinner."*

Somehow I held it in. And stepped up beside her as the chorus began to sing the second curtain song.

"Have a haunted haunted Christmas,
And a scary New Year's, too.

Have a haunted haunted Christmas,
And to one and all say, BOO."

We made it through the song once. But Mr. P was frowning and shaking his head. "It needs to be crisper," he said. "Crisper and a lot faster. Let's try it again."

So we started to sing again. And we were halfway through the song when I glanced up and saw the twin boys at the stairs again. They had their eyes on me. And as I sang, they raised their hands and pointed. Beckoned me with their fingers.

And that's when I lost it.

I couldn't hold it in any longer.

I screamed: "There they are! Don't you see them? Flora's twin brothers! There — on the stairs. Look! Can't you see them?"

Everyone stopped singing instantly. A hush fell over the room.

Everyone turned to the stairway. And the silence was quickly broken by laughter. And a lot of mumbling and low murmurs.

"I see them! I see them!" Courtney exclaimed. "Oooh, they're scary! Scary ghosts!"

Everyone laughed. Such a lame joke, but everyone laughed anyway.

The twins stared hard at me, their faces blank, no expression at all. Their dark eyes glowing coldly.

"I'm serious!" I cried. "I'm serious. They're standing right there!"

"Calm down, Kate," Mr. P said, motioning with both hands.

But I couldn't calm down. I had to let them know what danger we were all in.

"It's Ned and Abe," I said. "The twin brothers. See? Flora's twin brothers!"

"Kate is writing her own play!" Courtney said. That got a big laugh.

I could see that no one believed me. In fact, *everyone* believed I was totally losing it.

I saw Jack shaking his head and laughing. Paco was laughing so hard, he was bent over, slapping his knees. Even Mr. P had a big grin on his face.

I couldn't take it anymore. I couldn't take their laughter.

I thought maybe . . . just maybe they would believe me this time. But . . . no way.

"Remember the fifth-grade overnight?" Courtney was saying. "The ghost turned out to be a white trash bag?"

"Ooh, scary!" someone shouted.

I turned away from them. I wanted to cover my ears and shut out their dumb jokes and laughter.

I pushed away from Courtney and DeCarlos. I don't know what I was thinking. I started to run to the stairway.

Maybe I thought I could chase the twins away. Maybe I wasn't thinking at all. I only wanted to escape.

I lowered my head and bolted toward the stairs.

I could hear the kids shouting behind me. I could hear Mr. P calling me back.

But I didn't turn around. I ran full speed from the front room.

I didn't see the bookshelf jutting out at the doorway. I didn't see the long wooden shelf poking out from the hall. I shot right into it. My head rammed into the sharp corner of the shelf.

"Owwwwww!"

I heard myself scream. Stunned, I felt the blazing pain shoot through my body. Down from my head, like a hundred explosions . . . the pain rippling over me, folding me up, bringing me to the floor.

And then . . . only darkness.

29

The light seemed bright at first. I blinked several times until my eyes adjusted.

I'd only been out for a short time. Less than a minute, I think.

I could still hear the kids laughing and hooting in the front room. I figured they didn't see me bomb into the bookshelf headfirst. I rubbed my forehead.

"Ow." It really hurt to touch it. I knew I'd soon have a nasty bump there.

I picked Carol Ann's Cubs cap up from the floor and jammed it onto my head. Should I go back into the front room? Rejoin the chorus?

No. I couldn't stand any more of their jokes.

I turned and started up the stairs. No sign of the twins. I still felt dizzy from my bookshelf accident. Shaky-legged. My head throbbed. I held the banister tightly as I pulled myself up the creaking steps.

I planned to go to my room. Crawl into bed. And then . . .

Then what, Kate?

Regroup.

Yes. That was the word. *Regroup.*

If they didn't want to believe that this house was haunted . . . fine.

No problem.

I could handle their jokes. I'd been handling the jokes since fifth grade.

It hurt a little to see Jack laugh at me. I kind of had a crush on him.

But . . . whatever.

No one wanted to believe it, but I do have a special talent. I can see ghosts.

This talent got me in a lot of trouble. But maybe I could use it to help the others. Maybe I could somehow help protect them from the ghosts in this house. The ghosts no one wanted to believe in.

I started down the hallway to my room. I ran one hand along the wall because I still felt dizzy. I pressed a palm against my forehead. I could feel a small bump there. But it wasn't bleeding.

I stopped outside the room. Did I hear voices? Was someone else upstairs?

I leaned against the door frame and listened.

Yes. Soft voices. A man and a woman. Nearby.

I took a few steps toward the sounds and saw an open door. Peering into the doorway, I saw steep steps leading up to a brightly lit area. An attic.

I crept up to the stairway. Yes. The voices were coming from the attic.

I took a step back. *Be sensible, Kate,* I warned myself. *Don't go up there.*

But I didn't listen to myself. Maybe I was still stunned by the ferocious bump on my head. Maybe I wasn't thinking clearly at all.

But I raised myself onto the first step, slid my hand over the slender wooden banister, and began to climb.

"Hello!" I called. "Who's up there? Hello?"

30

"Whoa."

Some of the stairs were broken. I had to grip the banister to keep from falling. The whole stairway seemed to tilt from side to side as I pulled my way up.

At the top I could see flickering shadows over an orange light. The reflection of a fire.

I was breathing hard by the time I made it to the top. Gazing into the flickering light, I gasped in surprise.

I stepped into a long, low, old-fashioned looking room. Orange and yellow flames danced in a wide fireplace. I saw dark wood furniture, a dining room table set with many plates and glasses, a wood-burning stove in the center of the room.

Who lives up here?

Cinders from the fire made my eyes burn. I wanted to see every detail, but my eyes kept watering over.

At the far end of the fireplace, I saw a scraggly, almost-bare Christmas tree. It was decorated with strings of popcorn and burning candles. A ragged, dried-out holly wreath was hung over the attic window at the end of the room.

Blinking, struggling to focus, I finally saw them. The two boys on their stomachs on the floor. The two ghost boys, Ned and Abe, raised on their elbows, concentrating hard on a board game.

"Hello?" I called.

They didn't look up.

Why didn't I run? Why didn't I get out of there as fast as I could? I guess I was still stunned from my accident. In some kind of shock.

As I let my eyes wander away from the two boys, a man and woman came into focus. She stood beside the dining room table. She was plump, round-faced, dark ringlets of hair falling to her shoulders. She wore a white apron over a simple gray dress that came down to the floor.

He was lanky, bone thin. He had scraggly brown hair parted in the middle and down the sides of his dark-stubbled cheeks. His eyes were red and sad. He had a weary look about him as he gazed at me from a stiff-backed wooden chair.

"Welcome home, Flora," the woman said. A smile broke out over her face, and I saw several missing teeth. "Welcome home, dear."

"N-no," I stammered. "I'm not Flora."

The twins continued their game. They rolled a pair of wooden dice and moved small pieces around a game board. They didn't look up.

"In time to celebrate Christmas," the man said. He had a scratchy whisper of a voice. He kept his watery red eyes on me. He didn't smile.

The fire crackled loudly. I took a few steps into the room.

"Do you . . . live here?" I asked.

"We *exist* here," the man corrected me.

"We don't live anywhere anymore," the woman said. She shook her head sadly. Her chins quivered above the high, lacy neck of her dress.

You don't live anywhere because you are ghosts.

I was standing in this attic talking to a family of ghosts. All by myself with these sad-looking ghosts. How dangerous was this? I couldn't even imagine.

The woman motioned me forward. "We are so happy you came back to us to celebrate Christmas."

"Came back to you? No —" I said.

"Christmas has always been a hard time of year," the man said, rubbing his narrow, bearded chin. "It's when we lost you."

"Please," I begged. "Listen to me. I'm not Flora. My name is Kate. Kate Welles."

The woman's smile didn't fade. She stretched out her arms and moved toward me. "Let me hug you. It's been so long."

"No!" I cried. I raised my hands as if trying to shield myself. "No — please. Listen to me. . . ."

The woman wrapped me in a hug. Pulled me into that huge gray dress. I felt myself disappear. I couldn't see. I couldn't breathe. It was as if she had jammed me into a heavy wool blanket.

"Please —" My voice was muffled, my face pressed into the rough fabric of her dress. "I . . . can't . . . breathe."

Did she plan to suffocate me?

Finally, she pulled back. Her arms slid away. I gasped for air.

"What a wonderful celebration we shall have," she said, beaming at me. She straightened her apron.

The boys finally glanced up from their game. I recognized Ned. His hair was longer than Abe's. "Flora," he said. "We are playing Parcheesi. Do you want to play the next game?"

"No," I said. "Stop calling me Flora. You know I am Kate."

I turned to see that the father had risen from his chair. He stood in front of the fireplace, shadows darting over his dark overalls. His eyes were narrowed on me. His expression was grim.

I gasped when I saw a long-bladed knife in his hand.

"Wh-what are you doing with that?" I stammered, pointing.

"I am going to carve the bird," he said softly.

I glanced around. I didn't see a turkey anywhere.

I took a step back. He didn't take his eyes off mine. He gripped the handle of the knife tightly in one fist. "It is time to carve the bird," he said again.

"No. Please —" I suddenly felt in terrible danger. "This isn't happening," I said out loud.

I turned to the stairway, my heart pounding. "I am so sorry. I have to leave now. Sorry. Really. But I . . . I can't stay."

Where are the attic steps?

Somehow, I got turned around. I thought the stairway leading down was behind me. But now I saw only solid wall.

I turned back into the room. *There is an attic door. The stairs lead down from the door.*

But I saw no door. No stairs.

I saw only solid wall all around.

There is no way out of here! I realized. *No escape.*

"Time to carve the bird," the man said, raising his knife.

31

The man moved toward me, the knife at his side. The boys watched from the floor, their faces calm, almost bored.

I swung around and slammed the wall with my fist. I knew the stairs had been there. I hadn't walked far into the room. The attic door and stairs *had* to be behind me.

But my fist hit solid plaster.

Suddenly, the wife stepped in front of her husband. "Put the carving knife down, Aaron," she said. "It isn't time to eat yet. We have to celebrate first."

Aaron nodded and set the knife down on the table. "Sorry, Peg. I guess I was hurrying us," he said. "It has been so long since we had Christmas dinner."

"First, we will sing carols," Peg said. "Then the children can sit on Father Christmas's lap."

Huh? Father Christmas's lap?

My eyes searched the four walls. I even examined the floor, looking for steps going down or perhaps some kind of trapdoor.

No. No way out.

"Stand up, sons," Peg said. "It's time to celebrate with Flora. You can finish your Parcheesi game later."

She turned to me. "Now, Flora, tell us — what is your favorite carol?"

I stared at her. All four of them were watching me. My mind spun.

How do I get out of this attic? How do I get away from here?

"I'm sorry. I ... need to get back to the others," I stammered.

Aaron shook his head. "No, you don't."

"But Mr. Piccolo will be looking for me," I said.

"No, he won't," Aaron answered.

Suddenly ... suddenly, I realized what was going on.

I ran into that bookshelf and hit my head. I knocked myself out.

I was still unconscious. Just like after Courtney and I fell down that trapdoor in the school auditorium. I was still out cold.

And dreaming.

Yes, I had to be dreaming this whole scene. An attic without a way out? That *had* to be a dream. Four ghosts living in such a cozy place, waiting for their daughter to return for Christmas?

A dream.

And so, I knew what I had to do. I knew the only way to escape these ghosts and their attic home. I had to wake myself up.

Wake up, Kate. Come on. Pull yourself out of this nightmare.

Wake up — now.

I shut my eyes. I gritted my teeth. I tightened every muscle as I concentrated.... Concentrated . . .

Wake up, Kate. You can do it.

Rise up from this. Pull yourself up. Wake up.

I knew this was the answer. I knew I could end this crazy dream.

When I open my eyes, they'll all be gone.

32

I opened my eyes.

And gazed at the ghostly family staring back at me.

The fire crackled behind them. The big carving knife rested on the edge of the dining room table.

Not a dream.

Nothing had changed. This was happening. This was real.

I was trapped here, trapped in this attic with these frightening ghosts who insisted on calling me Flora.

A shiver went down my back. My knees started to fold. I forced myself to keep standing.

Stay alert, Kate. There has to be a way to escape.

"Sing a Christmas song for us, Flora," Peg said. "Sing something nice."

"They were singing new Christmas songs downstairs, Ma," Ned said.

"Yes, we listened to the new songs," Abe said.

Peg's smile grew wider. "Go ahead, Flora. Please. Sing us a new Christmas song."

I swallowed hard. My mouth was suddenly dry as cotton.

"Sing! Sing! Sing!" The twins jumped up and down and chanted.

My brain totally froze. Which song should I sing? I didn't really know them all by heart yet.

"Sing! Sing! Sing!"

"Okay," I said, motioning for them to settle down. "Here's one of the new songs from our show."

I took a deep breath and began to sing:

"Have a haunted haunted Christmas,
And a scary New Year's, too.
Have a haunted haunted Christmas,
And to one and all say, BOO."

"STOP!" Aaron screamed. "Stop singing that horrible song!"

I looked at the two boys. Their mouths had dropped open in shock.

Peg started to cry. Big tears ran down her cheeks. "That song has made me very sad," she said. "Why did you sing a song that makes fun of us? Why did you sing a hurtful song? Didn't you know how bad it would make us feel?"

"S-sorry," I stammered. "I . . . didn't think."

142

How could I have been so stupid? They didn't want to hear a funny Christmas ghost song. They were ghosts! They were dead. It wasn't a funny song to them.

"Really. I'm very sorry," I repeated.

Peg mopped the tears off her cheeks with both hands.

Aaron shook his head, his eyes on the floor. Both boys remained silent.

"Let's not spoil this special day," Peg said finally. "It's time for you kids to sit on Father Christmas's lap."

The boys clapped their hands. "Will Father Christmas bring us presents this year?" Abe asked.

"Our special present is to have Flora back," Peg said. She grinned at me lovingly. "Flora, since it's your special day, you can be the first to sit on Father Christmas's lap. Be sure to tell him all the gifts you would like this year."

What did she mean? I knew that Father Christmas was what they used to call Santa Claus back in the day. But how could I sit on his lap?

It didn't take long to find out.

Aaron disappeared into a closet at the back of the room. A short while later, he came out pushing a tall-backed chair. It was like a throne. And seated in the chair was a figure in a red-and-white Santa Claus suit.

Beneath the Santa hat, his head was tilted forward. So I couldn't see his face. At first, I thought it was a large puppet, some kind of mannequin. But as Aaron pushed the tall chair across the attic to me, I could see the bony hands and then the dull, yellowed skull.

And I realized I was staring at a human skeleton. A skeleton dressed in a wooly red Santa costume. The red coat was tattered and stained. One sleeve had nearly torn off. And the pants sagged, bony knees poking through holes in the fabric.

"This is one of our favorite traditions," Peg said, clasping her pudgy hands in front of her apron. "Father Christmas pays us a visit every year."

"Can I sit on his lap now?" Abe pleaded.

"No. Me," his twin insisted.

Peg pushed them back. "I told you, Flora will go first this year." She turned to me. "Go ahead, Flora. Sit on his lap. Tell him your Christmas wishes."

I swallowed hard again. I squinted at the grinning skull, tilted forward beneath the ratty cap. And as I stared, I saw the eyes move.

I gasped.

No. Wait. The eyes weren't moving. Something was moving inside the empty eye sockets.

"Sit on his lap, Flora," Peg urged. "You know you look forward to it."

Yes. Something inside the open eye sockets. Worms. Fat brown worms curling and uncurling where the eyes used to be.

"Sit down, Flora. Don't keep everyone waiting."

Peg's voice was becoming strained, harsh. She gave me a gentle push toward the chair.

I stood frozen as a long brown worm lowered itself from Father Christmas's nostril. And then another worm curled out from the grinning, toothless mouth.

"N-no . . ." I stammered.

"Go on, dear." Peg gave me another gentle shove. I stumbled over something on the floor. My arms shot out as I fell forward.

I fell headfirst onto the wormy skeleton. My face pushed into the scratchy wool jacket. My hands grabbed the hard shoulder bones.

It smelled. Oh, it smelled. My face buried in the jacket, I inhaled the odor of death. So sour and thick and strong. I felt like I was drowning in it, drowning in the putrid aroma.

I squeezed the arms and tried to pull myself up. But the arm bones *cracked off.* The arms slid off the shoulders. And my face dove into the bony chest again.

"Help me . . ." My cry was muffled by the scratchy jacket. "Oh, help . . ."

A few seconds later, I felt strong hands lifting me off the disgusting skeleton. Aaron stood me on my feet, then backed away. His face was set in a hard scowl.

The smile had faded from Peg's face, too. Her eyes were cold. She sneered at me. "Don't disappoint us, dear. We get angry when we're disappointed."

33

Her words sent a shiver to the back of my neck.

She seemed like a nice, enthusiastic mother, eager to enjoy the holiday. But I was frightened by her hard expression, the way she scowled at me so impatiently, so angrily.

This wasn't a happy family. These were dead people. And I was trapped here in this attic with them.

What would they do to me if I kept disappointing them?

Aaron pushed Father Christmas's chair back to the closet. The skeleton head bobbed as the chair bumped along the floor.

The boys shook their heads at me, frowning, as if they couldn't understand why I hadn't sat on the wormy skeleton's lap.

"Never mind," Peg said finally. She wiped her hands on the front of her apron. She forced a smile. "Let's have our Christmas dinner."

The boys hurried to the dining room table. Peg motioned for me to follow them. "Sit wherever you like, dear. I hope you are hungry."

No. I wasn't hungry. In fact, my stomach felt hard as a rock.

I took a seat across from the twins. Aaron stood at the head of the table. He picked up the carving knife. He ran a finger down the blade.

He lowered his eyes to me. "Turkey is your favorite — isn't it." It didn't sound like a question. It sounded like a threat. He ran his finger along the knife blade again.

"Here comes the turkey!" Peg announced cheerily. She carried a big oval platter to the table and set it down in front of her husband.

I gazed at the platter — and nearly choked.

I was staring at a turkey skeleton. All bones. No meat.

A short while later, Peg set a big bowl on the table in front of me. "Help yourself, dear," she said.

I peered into the bowl. I saw a big dust ball inside.

Another bowl appeared. Peg placed it on my other side.

I didn't want to look inside it, but I couldn't help myself. When I saw the pile of mouse heads in the bowl, I wanted to scream. My stomach did a flip-flop. I clapped a hand over my mouth to keep from puking.

I looked away. But I couldn't get the sight of the tiny black eyes in the furry gray mouse heads from my mind.

"Go ahead, dear," Peg urged. "Help yourself to my sweet potatoes." She pushed the bowl with the mouse heads toward me. "Taste it. Let me know if it needs salt."

"No. Really," I murmured. I felt my stomach heave again. "No thank you. I'm . . . not hungry. I —"

"*Taste it!*" Peg screamed. She raised a big serving spoon to my face. I stared at the two wilted mouse heads staring back at me on the spoon. "Taste it!"

She pushed the spoon to my mouth.

"Taste it. *Taste* it — *now!*"

34

"NOOOOO!"

I screamed and shot my hands up. I knocked the bowl away.

It crashed to the floor, and the mouse heads rolled out like little tennis balls.

I jumped to my feet. "You have to let me go!" I cried. I tried to walk away, but I stumbled over the mouse heads. The heads rolled all over the floor. I caught my balance against a dining room chair.

"You have to let me go back to the others," I said. "Back downstairs. You can't keep me here."

I stood with my hands pressed against my waist, breathing hard.

Peg pretended she didn't hear me. She wiped her hands again on her apron. I could see she was struggling to keep the anger off her face.

"Well, if you're not hungry, dear," she said, calmly, slowly, "let's open our presents now."

The twins cheered and clapped their hands.

Peg disappeared for a moment. Then she returned carrying a big gift box. She handed it to Aaron, who still sat at the head of the table.

"What could this be?" he said, running his hands along the red ribbon tied on the box.

He slid the ribbon off and pulled open the lid. His eyes went wide as he pulled out a ragged brown sweater covered with gaping moth holes. "A sweater!" he cried. "I love it!"

Peg smiled at him and patted his shoulder. "I know you do," she said. "I've given it to you every Christmas for over a hundred years."

They both chuckled as if she had made a funny joke.

Aaron held the ragged sweater up to show it off to Abe and Ned.

Peg turned to me. "And what did *you* bring us, Flora?"

My mouth dropped open. "Excuse me?"

"What did you bring us?" Peg repeated. "The boys are *dying* for some new presents."

They all laughed.

"*Dying*, see?" Peg said. "*Dying* for presents. That's a joke."

I didn't know what to say. I didn't think it was very funny.

This was insane. Like a terrible nightmare. Only, I knew I wasn't dreaming. I was trapped here with them. No way to escape.

I was totally at their mercy.

They waited for me to say something. Did they really expect me to bring them presents? My stomach tightened into a knot. I could feel the panic sweep over me, freeze me in place.

"We are waiting," Aaron said.

I shrugged. I lowered my head. "I . . . I don't have any presents," I said in a whisper.

They remained silent for a moment. No one moved. It was as if someone had pushed STOP and the video had frozen in place.

And then they began to change. Their faces reddened, then darkened to purple. Their dead eyes bulged. Their cheeks blew in and out like frogs' cheeks.

"You spoiled our Christmas!" Aaron growled. His purple face appeared ready to explode. He opened his mouth in an animal howl.

"You ruined *everything*!" Peg rumbled in a harsh, gravelly rasp. "You spoiled our holiday."

The boys changed, too. Their faces bellowed in and out. Like fish heads. Their eyes appeared about to fly out of their sockets. Their hair stood up on end. Straight up in the air. Their hands swelled. Their whole bodies shimmered and pulsed angrily.

"You spoiled Christmas," Peg roared. "You must be *punished*."

"No, please." I struggled to back away. But there was nowhere to go.

"Please," I begged. "What are you going to do? What are you going to do to me?"

35

"Punished," Aaron murmured. "You must be punished."

"No, please —"

The two boys moved toward me, dark eyes bulging. Their red faces pulsed in and out. They walked stiffly, like robots or zombies.

I tried to back away, but I was pinned against the attic wall.

"Punished," they chanted. "Punished."

Once again, the boys grabbed me by the arms. They gripped me with inhuman strength.

"Let go!" I cried. "Let go of me!"

I tried to squirm free. But they were too strong. They lifted me off the floor.

I kicked them. Squirmed and kicked.

But they weren't human. They didn't even look like boys anymore. More like red-faced, snarling monsters.

"Let *go* of me!" I kicked. I twisted. I tried to duck out of their grasp.

But they held me tightly under my arms. Above the floor. Nearly a foot off the floor.

Held me helpless. And carried me across the attic, past the dining room table with its skeleton turkey. Past the fireplace . . . the Christmas tree with its old-fashioned popcorn and burning candles . . .

To the attic window.

"Punished . . . Punished . . ." I could hear Aaron and Peg chanting in low voices behind me.

The boys pushed the wreath out of the way. Then they slid open the attic window. Slid it open all the way.

I could see a black-shingle roof tilting below the window. And beyond it — far below — the backyard with its garden shed, run-down shack, and stone well.

I could see it all through the open window.

"Punished . . . Punished . . ."

Without a groan, without a sound, the boys raised me higher. They lifted me to the open window.

"Hey — stop!" I screamed. "What are you doing? Let me down! *Stop!*"

They didn't react to my screams. Their eyes remained straight ahead. Their expressions didn't change.

"Good-bye, Kate," Aaron called. "Good-bye!"

The boys hoisted me higher — and heaved me out the attic window.

36

I sailed into the air. Too terrified to scream.

The cloudless blue sky seemed to lower itself to meet me.

My heart felt about to explode in my chest. I could feel the blood pulse at my temples.

But the shock of the cold air jolted me alert.

I landed on my back on the slanting roof below the window. Without thinking, I tucked my head and did a forward roll. It took me to the edge of the roof.

I could see the steep drop below me. Too far to jump down. I shot out both hands — and wrapped them around the metal gutter at the corner of the roof.

Swinging my body around, I held on to the drainpipe. Wrapped my legs around it. And slid . . . slid slowly down to the ground.

I took a few steps. My legs felt weak. Trembly. I struggled to catch my breath.

Have I escaped them? Have I really escaped?

I turned to the house. The lights were on in the kitchen. I could see some kids inside through the back window.

I have to warn my friends, I thought. *I have to tell them the ghosts are living upstairs.*

I fought off my dizziness and forced my legs to move. I took a few stumbling steps toward the kitchen when the sky suddenly darkened.

No. Not the sky. Abe and Ned flew down in front of me and slid beside me.

"Go away!" I cried. I tried to run.

But they grabbed me once again. Held me tightly under my arms.

Their parents loomed up in front of me. Frightening creatures now. Their faces twisted and distorted, like red, melting candle wax. As if they couldn't keep their shape. Their anger was so hot, it was *melting their faces*!

"You cannot escape, Kate," Peg rasped in an ugly animal growl. "You ruined our Christmas."

"You're ruining MINE!" I screamed.

A crazy thing to say. But I wasn't thinking clearly. How could I? I was insane with fear.

Their faces bubbled like hot tomato soup. Like the ugliest horror-movie monsters.

Had they once been a happy, caring family? It was hard to imagine.

Without a word, the boys lifted me off the ground again. They floated silently, carrying me across the backyard.

156

Gusts of wind swirled dead leaves beneath us. Bare trees shook their dark limbs, as if trying to warn us away. At the back of the yard, two crows perched on the wood fence. Both cawed hoarsely, flapping their black wings as we approached.

And then, there we were. We stood beside the stone well. The two monstrous parents. The strong, silent twins, their steel-like hands digging into my skin.

I tensed my whole body. I gritted my teeth so hard, my jaw ached and throbbed.

I couldn't fight them. I couldn't free myself.

As the parents watched, the twins raised me over the top of the well.

Gripped in terror, my senses went on super-alert. I could see every crack in the stone walls. I could see a tiny white worm crawling along the round wall edge. I could see ripples in the dark water far below.

Ned and Abe held me over the gaping opening.

I shut my eyes. "Please..." I begged. "Please..."

"Flora needs company for Christmas, too," I heard Peg say. "Please wish her a merry Christmas."

"Good-bye, Kate," the twins said in unison.

I felt their hands loosen their grip on me and slide away.

37

I felt myself start to slip down.

"WAIT!" I screamed. "I can *help* you!"

What was I thinking? I don't know. It was my last frantic attempt to save my life.

"I can help you!" I screeched.

The twins' strong hands tightened around me again. Slowly, they lifted me up, away from the well opening, and set me down on the ground.

I stood there, sputtering, shaking, hugging myself, trying to get it together. My brain whirred. My head throbbed.

The four of them huddled together in front of me. They didn't move. Their eyes locked on me, like cold lasers. They waited for me to speak.

Suddenly, miraculously, I had an idea.

"What if I bring Flora up from the well?" I said in a tiny, trembling voice. "What if I rescue her?"

They still didn't move. The parents' faces

bubbled and blistered. The twins didn't blink, just stared straight ahead like robots.

"What if I bring Flora up to spend Christmas with you?" I repeated. "If I do, will you let me return to the other kids?"

Aaron made a grunting sound. "Can't be done," he growled.

"But if I do it . . . ?" I said.

"If you rescue Flora, we will let you go back to them," he said in a hoarse whisper. "But it can't be done."

Peg raised her hands to her bubbling, melting cheeks. "Can't be done," she agreed.

How did I plan to rescue Flora?

I didn't have a clue. I was just stalling them, just trying to save my life.

Maybe . . . maybe I can find a way to get back to the others inside.

Maybe I can trick these ghosts . . .

"How long will you give me?" I asked. "I think I can rescue Flora. But how long will you give me to try? A day? Two days?"

If they give me a day, I can run inside to safety.

"Do it now," Aaron said.

"N-now?" I stammered. "No. I'll need a little time. I —"

He slid up to me, his eyes angry in that angry red face. "Now," he repeated. "Do it now."

"But — but —" I sputtered.

"Now."

This wasn't working out.

I needed a plan. I needed —

Whoa. Wait a minute.

Mr. Piccolo said the story of Flora and the ghosts had been passed down in his family. That story gave him the idea for his Christmas play. He said he had made one big change to the story. Because it was a Christmas play, he had Flora rescued in the end.

Yes!

And how was she rescued? By twelve screams. Someone screamed, "Come up!" twelve times — and Flora rose up from the bottom of the well.

Of course, that was just in Mr. P's play. But what if it really worked?

What if twelve screams could make Flora rise up from the bottom of the well and return to her family?

I had no choice. It was the only idea I had. I had to try it.

My life depended on it.

I turned to the well. I took a few steps toward it. I peered over the side.

I could see that still, dark water far below. A perfect black circle, smooth and black.

My legs were trembling. I was too terrified to breathe. Could I scream? Could I make a sound?

I took a step back. I cupped my hands around my mouth — and I started to scream.

"Come up! Come up! Come up . . . !"

My voice echoed down the well walls. "Come up! Come up! Come up!"

Carefully, I counted. Carefully, I numbered each scream.

It had to be twelve. The twelve screams of Christmas. Just like in Mr. P's play.

"Come up! Come up! Come up!"

I counted . . . ten . . . eleven . . . *twelve times I screamed*!

And then, gasping for breath, my chest heaving up and down, dizzy . . . suddenly so dizzy . . . I staggered back — and watched. Gazed at the top of the well. And waited . . .

Waited . . .

Would it work?

Would Flora come sailing up from her watery grave?

Aaron, Peg, and the two boys hovered close behind me. No one spoke. The only sounds were the caws of the crows and the whoosh of the gusting wind across the backyard.

And I could hear my heartbeat as I stared at the well. Stared and waited . . .

Flora? Are you coming up?

No. Silence from the well.

I took a deep breath, stepped up to the side, and peered down.

At the well bottom, the pool of black water stood still. Not a ripple. Not a splash.

No. No. No.

It didn't work.

I shut my eyes and backed away.

Those twelve screams would be my last.

38

And then I heard a soft splash. Just a whisper.

At first, I thought it was the rush of wind.

Another splash made me open my eyes. The sound came from deep in the well.

I turned but didn't move toward it. Afraid to see. Afraid that maybe I was imagining it because I was so frightened and desperate.

But wait. I heard another sound ring up from deep down below. A slap against the stones. Another splash. And then a steady *slap slap slap*.

I couldn't hold back any longer.

I dove to the side of the well. Gripped the cold stone wall and peered down.

I blinked as I saw a circle of red moving up from the darkness. It took me a while to focus and see that it was a red cap. Water spilled off the sides of the cap, sliding back to the black pool on the bottom.

I saw two pale hands slapping the sides of the round wall. Two hands and then the slender

arms poking out of a black dress. A young girl.
Flora. Climbing slowly. Climbing up the side of
the well.

Yes! Yes!

Water poured off her dress, off her dark shoes.
Inch by inch, she clawed and pulled herself up
the stone wall. I couldn't see her face. It was hidden by the floppy, red cap.

I realized I had stopped breathing. I let my
breath out in a long whoosh.

A wave of happiness and relief swept over
me. *You can relax now, Kate. You have rescued
Flora. You are safe now. The ghost family will
let you return to the others.*

But I couldn't relax — not until Flora was out
of the well.

Slowly, steadily, she climbed. And then she
stopped several feet below me.

She stopped and raised a pale hand to me.
"Pull me up." Her voice sounded watery, muffled, frightened.

"I can go no further," she said. "Pull me up.
Please hurry."

She clung to the wall with one hand. The other
she raised toward me, the little fingers curling and uncurling. "I've waited so long. Please
pull me up."

Forgetting the danger of the crumbling wall, I
leaned over and reached for her. I stretched my

arm down as far as it would go. Tried to stretch my hand to meet hers.

But I couldn't reach her. She was just a few inches too far down.

"Pull me up," she repeated, her voice shrill now, impatient. "Hurry. Pull me up." Her hand slapped the stones.

I tried again.

No. My hand wrapped around nothing but air.

"Come up a little higher," I called. "Just a few inches higher, and I can grab you."

"Pull me up," she said again. "I've climbed as high as I can climb. You must pull me up."

I leaned farther into the well. My waist was over the side. I stood on tiptoes. And reached . . . stretched my arm and reached down. And —

Yes!

My hand wrapped around hers. I felt the shock of how cold her hand was, how cold and soft and damp. Like a small fish.

"Pull me up," she said.

I tightened my fingers around her hand and tugged. I expected her to be light. I'm not sure why. I guess because she was a ghost.

But she had the weight of all the water soaked in her clothes.

She wrapped her fingers around my wrist and held tight. I tugged again. Leaned farther. Pulled with all my strength.

"Whoa." I lost my balance. Tumbled forward.

"NOOOO!" My scream echoed off the well walls as I started to plunge headfirst.

"Flora! Let go of me!" I shrieked. "Let *go!* *You're pulling me down!*"

39

Her hand slipped off mine.

I gaped in horror at the black pool below. I pushed my hands forward frantically — and pressed them to the wall.

I heaved myself backward, out of the well. My shoes thudded the ground. I felt my breath escape in a loud whoosh.

I bent over, hands on my knees, struggling to breathe.

A close call. A very close call.

Before I could turn back to the well, I heard Flora's muffled cry: "Pull me up. Hurry. Pull me up."

I peered into the well. She hadn't fallen back into the water. She clung to the side with both hands. Once again, she raised a tiny white hand toward me. "Pull me. Please. Don't leave me here."

"But I can't reach you!" I cried.

"Pull me. Pull me up."

"My arm — it isn't long enough," I said. "And I'm not strong enough, Flora. You'll pull me into the well."

"Pull me up. Pull me up."

I stood hunched over the side, peering down at her. The red cap tilted over her hair. Her long dress limp and wet. Her tiny hands pressed against the stones.

What can I do?

Her family hovered beside me. Their faces were tense and angry.

"Pull her up," Aaron ordered. "Now! Don't disappoint us again."

I stood frozen, listening to the little girl's frantic cries. And then I heard a shout. A girl's voice coming from the other end of the yard.

I spun away from the well. And watched the figure running toward me.

"Courtney!" I cried.

"I thought I saw you out here, Kate," she said breathlessly. "What are you doing here? Why are you back at the well?"

She didn't see the ghost family. *Of course* she didn't see them. I knew I didn't have time to explain to her. Besides, what was the point?

"Courtney — please help me," I pleaded.

She narrowed her eyes at me. "Are you okay? You look totally weird."

"I . . . I'll explain later," I said. "I need your help. Really."

She scrunched up her face. "What kind of help?"

"It's going to sound crazy," I said. "I'm going to lean over the side of the well, and I need you to hold my feet."

"No way!" she cried, taking a step back. "Are you *crazy*?"

"Please," I begged. "I need to reach something in the well. Just do this one favor for me."

She eyed me suspiciously. "This has something to do with ghosts — doesn't it."

"Yes," I said. "But there's no time to explain. Please. It's a matter of life or death."

She laughed. "Life or death for a *ghost*? You need help, Kate. I mean, like, a head doctor. Seriously."

"Pull me up," Flora called from inside the well. Aaron and Peg moved toward me menacingly.

I had to act. I couldn't wait for Courtney to agree. I spun back to the well. I lowered my head, leaned over far . . . reached my hand toward Flora's hand.

I grabbed it.

Once again, I tried to pull her up. And once again, I felt the tug of her weight. Felt my feet leave the ground . . . felt myself start to drop headfirst into the well.

Please, Courtney. Please grab my shoes. Please . . . do the right thing — for once.

She did.

I felt her hands wrap around my ankles.

"Pull!" I shouted to her. "Pull!"

In my tight grip, Flora began to slide up the side of the well.

Yes. Yes!

Her hat appeared over the top. And then her pale, smiling face, her dark hair dripping with water. I grabbed her around the waist. Squeezed tight. And hoisted her onto the ground.

Courtney shook her head in confusion. "What's going on here, Kate? This is nuts. What are you trying to prove?"

I didn't answer. I watched Flora's family rush to hug her. They were together again after more than one hundred years. I felt tears running down my cheeks. It was such an amazing, wonderful moment.

I turned to see Mr. P and the other kids come out of the house. Seeing Courtney and me, they started running to us.

Flora pulled herself from her family and floated over to me. She covered me in a wet hug. "Thank you," she whispered. "Thank you for rescuing me."

And then she turned to Courtney. "I have to thank her, too," she said to me. "I'm going to let her see me."

Flora walked up to Courtney. I saw a flash of light.

Courtney's eyes bulged.

"Thank you for rescuing me," Flora told her.

Courtney opened her mouth in a shrill scream. "A ghost! It's a *ghost!*" she shrieked.

Mr. P and the other kids stopped and stared.

"A ghost!" Courtney screamed. "I see her. I see a ghost!"

Kids began to laugh and hoot. They saw nothing but air.

"Whoa, Courtney," Jack called. "You're the new Ghost Girl!"

That made kids laugh even harder.

I had to smile. In a strange way, I had my revenge.

40

I enjoyed the rest of our stay in the old house. The play rehearsals were fun. There were no more visits from ghosts. Everyone kept teasing Courtney and calling her Ghost Girl.

Trust me, I hated to see the weekend end.

But Sunday night, we said good-bye to the haunted house, piled into the school bus, and bounced our way home.

Courtney wasn't in a great mood. She was finally seeing how it felt to be teased and made fun of all the time. I felt totally relieved. Like a new person. I couldn't have been happier to pass the title of Ghost Girl on to her — forever.

We sang the songs from the play all the way home . . .

"Have a haunted haunted Christmas,
And a scary New Year's, too.
Have a haunted haunted Christmas,
And to one and all say, BOO."

The bus stopped at my house. I grabbed my bag and ran up the driveway. Mom and Dad met me at the door. "How was it? How was the old house? How did rehearsal go? Did you have fun?"

They had a million questions.

By the time I'd answered them all — leaving out the ghost part, of course — I was ready for bed. I dropped my bag on the floor in my room. I felt too tired to unpack it.

I yawned. "It can wait till morning," I said aloud.

"*What* can wait till morning?" a voice asked.

I turned to the door — and saw a floppy, red cap. It tilted up and I saw Flora's face beneath it. She floated into my room, all dry now.

"Huh?" I gasped. "Flora? What are you doing here?"

She offered a sweet smile. "I decided to stay with you," she said.

"No — wait a m-moment," I stammered. "Flora — your family? What about your family?"

"I like you better," she said. "They left me in the well for over a hundred years. What kind of family is *that*?"

"But — but —"

She smiled again. She had tiny dimples in her cheeks when she smiled.

"We'll have such good times together," she

173

said. "When do we go to school? I can't *wait* to meet your friends."

"No. Flora, bad idea. Wait —"

She tossed the red cap onto my bed. "But, Kate — there's only one bed. Where will *you* sleep?"

Goosebumps
MOST WANTED

A NIGHTMARE ON
CLOWN STREET

Here's a sneak peek!

Heather and I sat across from each other at my kitchen table. We had a bowl of nacho chips and a bowl of pretzels in front of us.

I could hear voices down the hall. My parents' book club was meeting in our den.

We couldn't agree on what our science project should be. I said we should do a study on invisibility and bring in an invisible project to school. That would be totally easy.

Heather rolled her eyes. She didn't like that idea.

I said, "We could do some experiments with different liquids. See which ones your dog Clyde will drink."

Heather hit the tabletop with her fist. "No way. I'm not giving Clyde weird things to drink."

"Even for an A in science?" I said.

"Shut up, Ray," she replied. "I think we should do something with soil."

"Huh? Soil? You mean like *dirt*?"

"We could get different kinds of soil and try to grow stuff in them," Heather said.

"You're kidding, right? Gardening? Why don't you just kill me now?" I groaned.

This was going nowhere. I had an idea that was better than working on this project. Actually, I'd been planning it all day.

I pushed my chair back and stood up. "Follow me," I said. I waved her toward the kitchen door.

Her green eyes flashed. "Where are we going?" she demanded.

I raised a finger to my lips. "Ssssh."

I could hear a woman reading something out loud in the den. I didn't want my parents to know Heather and I were going out. It's no fun to sneak out if people know about it.

I pulled open the kitchen door. The warm evening air blew in. "We'll have an adventure," I said.

"No. Really," Heather said. "We have to stay and work on this project. We're already late, and we don't have a clue."

But I stepped out into the backyard. I knew Heather would follow me.

The air felt hot, as if I'd stepped into an oven. My parents keep the air conditioning cranked up pretty high. The sun had just gone down. The sky was streaked gray and purple. A bird cooed from somewhere in the lemon tree at the back of the yard.

Heather bumped me from behind. "Where are we going, Ray?"

"It's a surprise," I said, moving along the side of the house toward the street.

"And we're doing this *because*?"

I turned back to her and whispered, "Because we're going to join the circus."

About the Author

R.L. Stine's books are read all over the world. So far, his books have sold more than 300 million copies, making him one of the most popular children's authors in history. Besides Goosebumps, R.L. Stine has written the teen series Fear Street and the funny series Rotten School, as well as the Mostly Ghostly series, The Nightmare Room series, and the two-book thriller *Dangerous Girls*. R.L. Stine lives in New York with his wife, Jane, and Minnie, his King Charles spaniel. You can learn more about him at www.RLStine.com.

Catch the MOST WANTED Goosebumps® villains UNDEAD OR ALIVE!

NEED MORE THRILLS?

GET Goosebumps!

WATCH
ON TV
ONLY ON
hub

PLAY
Wii

ON DVD

LISTEN

The Original Bone-Chilling Series

—with Exclusive Author Interviews!

NIGHT of the LIVING DUMMY

R.L. STINE

DEEP TROUBLE

R.L. STINE

MONSTER BLOOD

R.L. STINE

The HAUNTED MASK

R.L. STINE

ONE DAY at HORRORLAND

R.L. STINE

the CURSE of the MUMMY'S TOMB

R.L. STINE

BE CAREFUL WHAT YOU WISH FOR

R.L. STINE

SAY CHEESE and DIE!

R.L. STINE

the HORROR at CAMP JELLYJAM

R.L. STINE

HOW I GOT MY SHRUNKEN HEAD

R.L. STINE

R. L. Stine's Fright Fest!
Now with Splat Stats and More!

REVENGE OF THE LIVING DUMMY
R.L. STINE
SCHOLASTIC

CREEP FROM THE DEEP
R.L. STINE
SCHOLASTIC

MONSTER BLOOD FOR BREAKFAST!
R.L. STINE
SCHOLASTIC

THE SCREAM OF THE HAUNTED MASK
R.L. STINE
SCHOLASTIC

DR. MANIAC VS. ROBBY SCHWARTZ
R.L. STINE
SCHOLASTIC

WHO'S YOUR MUMMY?
R.L. STINE
SCHOLASTIC

MY FRIENDS CALL ME MONSTER
R.L. STINE
SCHOLASTIC

SAY CHEESE – AND DIE SCREAMING!
R.L. STINE
SCHOLASTIC

WELCOME TO CAMP SLITHER
R.L. STINE
SCHOLASTIC

THE SCARIEST PLACE ON EARTH!

HELP! WE HAVE STRANGE POWERS!
R.L. STINE

ESCAPE FROM HORRORLAND
R.L. STINE

THE STREETS OF PANIC PARK
R.L. STINE

WHEN THE GHOST DOG HOWLS
R.L. STINE

LITTLE SHOP OF HAMSTERS
R.L. STINE

HEADS, YOU LOSE!
R.L. STINE

WEIRDO HALLOWEEN
R.L. STINE

THE WIZARD OF OOZE
R.L. STINE

SLAPPY NEW YEAR!
R.L. STINE

THE HORROR AT CHILLER HOUSE
R.L. STINE

Goosebumps® Hall of Horrors

THERE'S ALWAYS ROOM FOR ONE MORE SCREAM!

An all-new series from fright-master R.L. Stine!

Goosebumps Hall of Horrors
CLAWS!
R.L. STINE

Goosebumps Hall of Horrors
NIGHT OF THE GIANT EVERYTHING
R.L. STINE

Goosebumps Hall of Horrors
SPECIAL EDITION!
THE FIVE MASKS OF DR. SCREAM
R.L. STINE

Goosebumps Hall of Horrors
WHY I QUIT ZOMBIE SCHOOL
R.L. STINE
SCHOLASTIC

Goosebumps Hall of Horrors
DON'T SCREAM!
R.L. STINE
SCHOLASTIC

Goosebumps Hall of Horrors
THE BIRTHDAY PARTY OF NO RETURN!
R.L. STINE
SCHOLASTIC